DEADLY THREAT

SCVC TASKFORCE ROMANTIC SUSPENSE SERIES, BOOK 13

MISTY EVANS

Deadly Threat, SCVC Taskforce Romantic Suspense Series, Book 13

Misty Evans

© 2021

ISBN: 978-1-948686-47-1

Print ISBN: 978-1-948686-48-8

Please Note

ACKNOWLEDGMENTS

It takes a village... In my case, sometimes it takes even more than that to help me create a story like Mia and Malachi's. I outlined this book nine months ago, but when I sat down to start typing, it wasn't the right story. Not even close.

I panicked. The book had a deadline and I needed a whole new plot. Then my friend, Karen, gave me the opening during one of our enormously fun Zoom chats. She didn't even realize it—nor did I at the time—but when I sat down to start the story the next day, determined to get at least one chapter done, bingo. Karen's words came pouring out of Mia's mouth. Thank you, my friend, for being a source of inspiration without even knowing it!

My eye has been having issues and I was six chapters in when my doctor told me I needed to limit my screen time. I do everything on the computer, and I was already weeks behind on this story because we were house hunting, my sons had come to visit, and other things kept popping up. Elisa, another friend and often an early reader, jumped right in to help. A rush job, I dictated as fast as I could and she transcribed just as quickly. Thank you, Elisa!

While writing the story, my editor and friend, Patricia, lost her beloved cat, Tazmania. Taz was a delight and I wanted to honor her, so I named Mia's cat after her. Thank you, Patricia and Taz, for being part of the SCVC Taskforce series.

Along with Taz, I needed information on therapy and emotional support animals. An author and friend, JB Lynn, supplied me with important details, since she has a therapy dog. She also kept me going when I felt like the story might kill me before I finally got through the draft. "You've finished a story before, you can do it again," she counseled. She was right (like always).

Nearing the climax of the story, Malachi argued with me about his injury. (Yes, I talk to my characters.) I had it all planned out, but it would leave him unable to compete in a competition near and dear to his heart, and he tried to talk me into making him a Jason Bourne-type character who could get up and walk away with barely a scrape. My medical expert, Maria Mercedes, confirmed that the injury would require surgery, put him out of commission for a long time, and would require extensive physical therapy afterward. Thank you, Maria, for your advice and sharing your knowledge with me. If you'd like to read the interview I did with Mia and Malachi after the story, please join my official reader group here: www.facebook.com/groups/223349495973783/ OR email misty@readmistyevans with MALACHI as the subject and I'll send it to you.

As always, I have so much gratitude to my readers who keep me inspired, especially my official Facebook fan group who picked the title of this story. It was as if some of you knew I needed a pep talk during the two months of work it took to draft it, and your emails and comments gave me a lift every day.

Just so you know, I save every piece of fan mail I receive, and love hearing from all of you.

There are others who contributed to story details, kept me fed, made sure I showered, and helped polish the story to make it shine. My husband, my cover artist, my assistant, and my editors deserve so much credit, and I thank you all. Hard to believe this is the 13th book in the series!

I hope you enjoy the story!

Misty

ONE

Threats, Mia Livingston had discovered, were everywhere.

Including those from her older sister.

"You'll never find your soulmate at the library," Amber chastised, her voice serious, even as she smiled and winked on screen, teasing. "You like those big, muscular jocks, sis. They don't get those bodies with their head stuck in books."

Mia grabbed her messenger bag and slung it on, maneuvering the phone and her arm through the strap. Her twelve pound terrier-mix bounced on her paws at the door, knowing they were going out. "I have a job. Professor Coggins needs info on ancient Egyptian medicines." Plus, Mia had no interest in finding her soulmate. They didn't exist, in her opinion, and relationships were off the table for her. Like, forever.

"Have you heard of the internet?"

Her sister was a Grade A smartass. "Believe it or not, there are older texts on the subject that no one has ever scanned and put on the World Wide Web." She rubbed Taz's head making the gingery undercoat shine through as she passed the tiny, aged feline lying in the sunny front window of the small apartment. The wide stripes of her tiger tabby coat rippling, the old girl purred and blinked at Mia, a paw gently patting her hand, as if saying thank you. "We're lucky the university library can access these editions for us."

"You're hopeless." Amber flopped down in the high-backed seat at her office.

"And *you* need to get laid." Mia clipped the non-retractable leash on Ladybug's harness and double-checked the vest with the certifying agency's logo on it. "Whenever you start chiding me about my love life, it's a sure sign you need to work on yours."

"You know me too well." Amber twirled, looking away from the view outside. Downtown San Diego, with its blue skies, high rises, and a few trees, now framed her head. The buzz of some machine sounded in the background and she grimaced. "I hate gyms. I also hate all this noise. I need to get out of here in order to work."

The mayor's office was getting a remodel, and soon Mia's sister would have to move temporarily from her semi-posh digs into another space during the renovation. "Come to the library. We have knowledge."

Amber laughed. "I may take you up on that."

It would be so good to see her in person. The thought made Mia smile. "But you like muscles and sweaty guys," she reminded her. *Just like I do.* "The gym is where you find such creatures, so suck it up."

"Says the sister on her way to the cave-like archives of a library." Amber made kissy noises at the dog. "Give her a hug for me."

Mia checked she had Ladybug's certification and proof of insurance; it was force of habit more than anything else. She *always* had the documents, but seeing them before she left the safety of her home helped keep some of the anxiety at bay. "She misses you. We all do."

"Let's have dinner tonight."

Mia faltered at the threshold, Ladybug halting as well, to cock her head. Mia took a deep breath, checked both ways, then stepped through. The canine followed and Mia pulled the door shut. Her hand rattled the knob, making sure it had locked. It had, but she checked again. "That's not a good idea."

Her sister sighed, the kind that sounded like she'd pulled it all the way up from her toes. "Mia, he's dead. Let's celebrate."

Mia hurried down the hall, the stink of stale beer and old carpet filling her nose. She hated this place, but who would look for her here? That's how she planned to keep it.

There was no one out and about yet in the building. She didn't glance at the screen as she headed for the stairs, Ladybug's small paws keeping pace. "I'm not celebrating a man's death," she said in a low voice.

The dog looked up at her and whined. Then she stopped, putting her body in front of Mia, so she couldn't take the next step. Mia faltered.

"He kidnapped, tortured, and nearly killed you," Amber reminded her. As if she needed such a thing. A well-manicured fingernail tapped on her desk. "I'm glad Marcher's dead, and now you're free of him and what happened. No more hiding. I want to be able to see you whenever I want, and tonight we're lifting a glass to your freedom."

The words reverberated through her—*kidnapped, tortured, killed.* The old alarm bells went off, Mia's pulse jumping. *No, no, no. Not now.*

Ladybug pawed at her leg and whimpered again. The sides of the stairwell seemed to close in on them, threatening to squeeze the air from Mia's lungs. She stopped, sitting down hard on the cool metal steps. "I can't do this right now."

Ladybug climbed into her lap and began licking her face. She could barely whisper. Her throat was closing up. "I have to... I have to go..."

Suddenly understanding that she'd triggered an anxiety attack, Amber panicked. "I'm sorry! I didn't mean to upset you. Please don't hate me. I thought you'd be happy, MiMi."

The nicknamed flowed like water over Mia's taut nerves. Ladybug, as usual, did her job, pressing her strong, warm body against Mia's chest and continuing to lick her.

Seconds ticked by. She focused on her breathing, like her therapist told her to. Mentally imagined open fields and wildflowers. Her fingers tangled in the terrier's fur, soft and wiry at the same time.

Her throat began to relax. The walls receded an inch. She took a breath, then another.

Amber's voice was distant, faint. Mia continued to breathe, dropped her face into Ladybug's fur. The walls fell back, the suffocating anxiety with them.

Her lungs expanded. The ringing in her ears subsided. Ladybug barked gently, as Mia lifted her face and blinked.

"Talk to me," Amber said. "Do you need an ambulance?"

Better but still shaking, Mia drew a deep breath and looked at her sister's horrified face onscreen. "I'm...okay."

"No, you're not. Forget the library. Go back to your apartment. I'll call Dr. Jeeves."

Mia squeezed her eyes shut and gritted her teeth. She hadn't had an attack in ages, and certainly not one that had come on so quickly. Tilting her head down to rub her face against Ladybug's once more, she forced her voice to sound stronger. "Don't." She lifted her head and put extra emphasis on the words. "*I'm okay.*"

There was no way she'd let Damon Marcher have power over her, especially in death. He'd been convicted, thanks to her testimony, but had tried to control her from prison. She'd been in witness protection before and after the trial. Bars or no, he'd been able to keep his men looking for her, wanting to use her against her sister.

She'd been his pawn for too long in the past seventeen months. Even after Mia had been rescued, even while under the U.S. Marshals' protection, she'd been in hiding and it sucked.

Now, with the leader of the Quattro Gang dead, and their group in tatters, Mia Livingston was mere history to them.

It was time they were the same for her.

She would never be anyone's pawn again, and she knew how to protect herself now. Didn't mean she didn't still have unusual fears and triggers, but she had to get over them, one way or another.

As she focused on continuing to breathe slow and steady, her sister stayed quiet and let her and Ladybug do their routine. When the last of the restriction left her lungs, she set the dog aside and stood. "There. All better."

"I'm so sorry," Amber stated again.

The words scratched like sandpaper against her skin, not because she blamed her sister. Not one bit. The fact that Mia wasn't the kickass person she used to be was what irritated her. That Amber would ever feel the need to apologize for anything did, too. "Please don't," she said, gripping the handrail. "It's not your fault. I have to be able to talk about it."

The fact she couldn't even hear Marcher's name without freaking out meant she wasn't doing as well as Dr. Jeeves believed. As well as Mia, herself, had hoped.

Which meant it *was* time for a session, but her next wasn't for two weeks.

She started down the stairs again, focusing on Ladybug's harness and the white *Therapy Dog* designation stamped on it.

She didn't want to take time from her new assignment to squeeze an emergency visit in. *I can handle this.*

"Can I please make this up to you tonight?"

"I have a meeting." The words flew out of her mouth before she even registered them. It was the perfect excuse, though. There was always a PTSD/peer group gathering at the Catholic Church not far from Amber's office on Tuesday evenings.

Meeting, it is. That might be enough to keep her from losing it until her appointment with Jeeves.

Amber nodded, expression desperate. "Afterward. I'll pick you up."

Mia hit the landing. Could she really see her tonight? Was she *really* free? "That's not necessary."

"It's at the church, right?"

"Are you keeping tabs on me?"

Amber looked slightly abashed. "I know the time and location of all the peer support groups meeting in the area." Big surprise. "I know you'd prefer the other members don't see me, in order to protect your identity. If it makes you feel better, I'll park a few blocks down."

Mia shifted back and forth on her feet. It had been so long. Marcher was dead. Could she reclaim this part of her life and see her family again? "I don't know."

"Baby steps. It won't be easy resurfacing after the last year and a half, but you can do it. I know you can. My dream of having you beside me *is* possible. We're focusing on the future, not the past, okay?"

The future. Once, Mia knew hers would be by Amber's side, all the way to the Oval. While Mia had never been a fainting wallflower, she'd never desired the pursuit of fame and power like her sister did. Yet, she'd always supported her. Since high school student council, Mia had written Amber's speeches, coordinated her campaigns. It was a dream job, assisting her to the mayor's office.

Damon Marcher had ruined that.

If only I hadn't gone out that night...

Mia opened the exit door, bright sunlight and the smell of fresh cut grass clearing the stagnant stairwell from her senses. Blaming herself wasn't the answer. "The future, right." She wouldn't celebrate the violence of Marcher's death, but maybe it was time to release what happened, as Amber was encouraging her to, and find her liberation. *I'm done being a victim. Done being afraid.* "I'll think about dinner. Let me see how today goes. Text me later."

"Are you sure you can handle going out right now?"

Mia forced a smile as she and Ladybug crossed the street to the WeGo ride waiting for her. She felt as safe at the university library as she did in her own place. The shelves of books, the scarred tables, the dry paper smell. She loved it. "I'll be fine."

"Call me if you need anything," Amber told her, still looking worried, but trying to hide it. "Or if you find your soul-mate amongst those worn out stacks of forgotten tomes."

Mia stuck her tongue out and disconnected. Later, once she was done with Coggins' research, she'd think about dinner. It felt good to at least entertain options.

"How are my girls?" Sue asked, reaching over the seat to pat Ladybug when Mia climbed in.

"She's great." A date with the library was better than anything these days. Maybe she wouldn't need the meeting tonight after all.

"Ready?" Sue shifted into gear.

Ladybug set her front paws on the door handle and stared out the window. "You know it. I have a good feeling about today, Sue. Let's go."

HER GOOD FEELING evaporated twenty minutes later when she coasted through the library, Ladybug at her feet, and a stack of old books weighing down her hands. She was prepared for a few blissful hours lost in the books, then she'd have Sue go through the drive-through at South of the Border, her favorite Mexican place, to pick up a tasty lunch on the way home.

When she rounded the corner, heading for her favorite table, she pulled up short.

Threat! Threat!

A man was sitting there.

No one ever sat in this section of the library at *this* table but her.

Headphones in and fingers pecking at the keys of a thin laptop, he didn't notice. She scanned him from head-to-toe, Ladybug glancing between the two of them.

His dark hair curled around his ears, several days' worth of beard covering a strong jawline. Dressed in a short-sleeved shirt and distressed jeans, he'd kicked the chair opposite him to the side to make more room for his legs.

His very long, muscled legs, that the jeans seemed to hug.

His biceps and forearms were no slackers either. They bulged with every click of the keypad. He wasn't a fast typist, but a decent one, only stopping here and there to reread the screen before he resumed.

Wait 'til I tell Amber, she thought, smugly. An attractive, muscle-bound guy—probably military, since this *was* San Diego and there were plenty of those around—who was in the library. He wasn't reading a book, but no matter. Amber hadn't specified that.

Mia ran an approving gaze over him again, catching herself

wondering if his brain matched the size of his biceps. *Whoa, there.* She tore her gaze away. She wasn't looking for a guy and this particular one had violated a big tenet right off the bat—he was in her seat.

Ladybug seemed confused, knowing that was where they always landed inside this huge place. It was a quiet corner in antiquities, and out of the way. Normally, the dog would nestle under Mia's feet for hours, content to sleep. Now she leaned into Mia's leg and kept glancing up as if asking what she should do.

Ladybug was scanning her to make sure she wasn't about to have another attack. While annoyed, and a tad confused herself about why her stomach was flip-flopping at the thought of confronting the man, no full-on panic pricked at her.

Yet.

It was a free country and he could sit anywhere he damn well chose. But here? This was her cave, her hideaway, and finding a different one, where she wasn't constantly interrupted by students or staff, could take valuable time. Part of controlling her overreactions to being in public was about managing her surroundings. She needed continuity and familiarity to feel safe.

As though he finally sensed her presence, McHottie glanced in her direction, and damn, those were some eyes.

Bluer than the contacts she sometimes wore, and she had no doubt it was his natural color. She'd left hers out today, showing her natural color, and it felt a bit...revealing. With his tan skin and dark hair, he looked like the sexy villain in some teen drama.

He popped out an earbud. "Can I help you?"

Boy, could you.

Except, *wait*, that was wrong. She was so not interacting with McHottie here. Nope, no way. She needed to unglue her traitorous feet that were stuck to the floor and move on. *Nothing to see here, folks.*

Without warning, her lips betrayed her, too. "That's my table."

He did a double-take: at her, the dog, the vest, and then the scarred wooden top his computer sat on. "I didn't realize you could reserve one."

"I'm special," she said. *Where had that come from?* "Never mind. I'll find someplace else."

He grinned and her mind went blank, feet and limbs still on strike and refusing to let her escape. "No need." He used his foot to hook the chair and bring it closer to the table. To him. He sat up straighter. "We can share. I'll be done in a few minutes and you can have it all to yourself."

Her pulse kicked. *Run*, it said. *Stay*, her body begged. *Threat*, her mind screamed.

She swallowed hard. The table beckoned to her, the words dozens of stupid college students had carved into it welcoming. The light was perfect, the chair hard but suitable. She felt safe in this spot.

Ladybug stood and tugged gently on her leash, leaning toward the guy.

Even the dog was a turncoat.

A few minutes. She could stand him for that long, right? Then the space would be hers once more.

Taking a focused breath, she found the old Mia, the one who would have marched to the seat without a hint of doubt, and slowly lifted a foot.

It moved. She did the same with the other.

Two more steps and she was within spitting distance. The man half-stood and leaned forward, reaching out to help her with the books. Her instinct was to pull back, but she didn't. She simply stopped, shook her head, and proceeded to put the volumes down herself. He seemed to respect her space and sat once more.

Ladybug scooted to her normal spot and Mia hesitantly sat, not in the chair the stranger had indicated, but next to it, farther from him by a few inches.

Control. She just had to retain a bit of it.

From under her lids, she noticed him hiding a smile as he returned to his typing. He didn't say a word about the dog, or ask questions about her choice of research material.

That was good.

He did, however, put his earbuds away and sneak a peek at her.

She made a show of fishing out her own laptop and opening her document. Then she ran through Coggins' list of questions. While she didn't catch him staring directly at her, she could sense every time McHottie chanced a glance her way.

Unfortunately, unless she jumped and ran, there wasn't a damn thing she could do about it.

And she was done running.

TWO

Malachi covertly watched the woman stack her books like a wall between them. She looked familiar, though he couldn't place the red hair and green eyes.

Sexy as hell, but he wasn't here to pick up some twenty-something college girl. Besides, she had issues. Who ever heard of *owning* a table at the library?

I'm special. Her words rang in his ears. Yeah, didn't everyone think that?

Her odd reaction to his presence was a tip off she had a screw loose. The dog gave substance to the theory, although he thought therapy dogs were trained for visiting nursing homes and schools. Maybe the scruffy terrier was her emotional support animal as well. One of his friends from the Corp had an ESA. The guy suffered from surreal nightmares and social anxiety.

Either way, her selection of reading materials confirmed his suspicions. He scanned the titles of the book wall: *Ancient Medicine: From the Beginnings of Civilization; Egyptian Medical Papyri Science and the Art of Healing;*

Plant, Animal, and Mineral Ingredients Used in Egyptian Medicine.

None of his beeswax, but her interests sounded like a yawn fest in the making.

Resuming his night classes in Behavioral Psychology had seemed to be the perfect way to fill his lonely evenings. Since both of his brothers had settled down, Mal had been twiddling his thumbs and ending up at his parents' house more days than not for dinner. His mother kept trying to set him up with women, and bless her heart, she didn't have a clue about who and what attracted him.

He'd thrown himself into training for the San Diego marathon, and that took plenty of time every day, but his brain needed to work. He needed something to think about while running, swimming, and biking, when it was just him and the road, water, and nothing else.

The flood of endorphins gave him the zen feeling he craved, but after the initial hour or so of exercise, his brain would start in on the woulda-coulda-shouldas, and old memories would surface. While he'd loved being a Marine, some of his missions had left mental scars and battle wounds he might never recover from.

His current college assignment, however, might dump his 4.0 GPA down into no-man's land. The final report was due next week and he hadn't even started. He needed a volunteer for a study, and he didn't have a single friend that fit the parameters.

So he'd made one up. As he typed the next bullshit line into his document, he tried to think like his fake guy, Homer. He'd just finished taking another of the online personality tests to get into character and answer the assessment quiz he'd designed himself.

Which was making his brain go in circles.

Maybe he should bribe one of the Taskforce members to help him out. Coop would never do it, but Thomas? That ball-buster loved a dare and could be bought off with a good steak and a bottle of AMASS Los Angeles Dry Gin.

He'd also give a bunch of crazy answers and make Malachi's analysis look as if a five-year-old wrote it. It sure would be interesting to peer into that guy's mind, though. A West Point grad with serious undercover work under his belt, he was probably more dangerous than most of the criminals the Cahill brothers brought to justice. He'd heard but never confirmed that Mann had done a stint with a spec ops unit, as if the rest of the package wasn't already a first class deal.

One of the books slipped from its lofty height and Malachi caught it. The woman startled, blinked, then accepted it from him as he handed it to her. "Thanks."

"What class is that for?" he blurted. Anything to keep from working on his assignment.

She glanced at the edition and flipped it open. "None. Just research."

"Going into medicine?"

Her petite brows dipped as she focused on the table of contents. "God, no. I'd be lousy at it."

"History?"

Her tentative gaze rose to his. "I thought you were almost done with whatever you're working on?"

Burned.

Her voice was soft and gentle but the brush off was there. He was no idiot and could take the hint, yet couldn't seem to help himself. He wanted to keep her talking, see those perfect cupid lips move again. Why was her face so familiar? "I think I'm in over my head."

The faintest of grins tugged at her mouth as she flipped past several chapters. "Aren't we all?"

Under the table, the animal moved and Mal glanced at it. He knew service dogs were off-limits, but therapy and ESAs were used to attention. "What's his name?"

She didn't miss a beat, her finger scanning a page. "Hers is Ladybug. Yes, she's a therapy dog, and yes, you can pet her, if you wish."

The answers were so automatic and pat, he knew she'd been asked a million times. He liked dogs, had thought about getting one. Maybe bring it to the office. Joe and Samantha had a dog; Caleb, his twin, and Josie had some cats. Malachi had to admit, he felt a bit left out, both with his lack of human companionship and that of any animals. His brothers had found their soulmates, and here he was, focused on a marathon and college courses. Although he was nearing thirty, he didn't want a relationship, didn't need it, either. But a dog? That he could do.

Ladybug's licorice eyes stared at him, her tail thumping against the woman's ankle when he smiled. She sat on her owner's foot and leaned into her legs.

Lowering his hand, he let her sniff it, then laughed when she gave him a lick. "You're a good girl, aren't you?"

Another lick and more wagging. He shifted a bit so he could scratch under her chin. She seemed to enjoy it and did a play bow, stretching out her body.

Big dogs were more his thing, but one this size might be easier to handle. He could travel with it, take it with him on surveillance or when he was going after a fugitive.

He could even train it to assist him with takedowns.

The click of typing met his ears. The woman had an assortment of colored sticky note pads out and she'd parked a pen in the crevice at the top of her ear. She scanned the open book page, marked it with a blue tab, then entered info into her laptop. Her fingers flew across the keyboard and he envied her that.

"You're a teacher's assistant, aren't you?" He repositioned his big body in the wooden chair that seemed normal, but felt like an elf chair with his bulk in it.

She didn't so much as blink. "Not quite."

It'd been a long time since he'd struck out with a woman, but he hadn't gotten one iota from her, except about the dog. Not that he was flirting or anything, but she would barely meet his eyes.

A research assistant of any kind could be a boon for him. If he could convince her to help him with his project...

Plus, he liked a challenge.

"I'm sorry I took your table," he offered, hoping to score some points. "My office was chaos this morning and I needed peace and quiet to work on an assignment." She glanced at him and he went on. "Yeah, I'm a little old for college, even as a grad student, but I enjoy learning, and taking a few night courses seemed to be a good idea at the time." He blew out a disheartened breath. "Unfortunately, my current class is kicking my butt. I really hate failure—as in *passionately* hate it—but I have to face facts. I'm going to fail this course."

She finished typing and closed the volume, shuffling it into the stack and drawing out another. "There's this thing called a tutor. You might you look into it."

Humor? That was unexpected. "Can you recommend one?"

Her saw her bite her bottom lip. Her hands paused before opening the book and she stared down at it, but didn't seem to be seeing it. "What are you taking?"

Yes. Gotcha. "I have a BA in criminal justice, but I've decided to go for a degree in behavioral science."

Eyes averted, she nodded, closed her laptop, then stowed it

and the colorful sticky notes into her bag. "Student services can suggest somebody." Without warning, she stood and gathered the books.

"Are you leaving?" He rose, too. "I apologized about the table. I'll go, you don't have to."

"It's not that," she said, going around him, the dog on her heels. "Good luck with your assignment."

Just like that, she was gone. Ladybug glanced back at him, scorn in her dark eyes, suggesting he'd messed up.

He almost followed them, apologized again, but kicked the table leg instead. *Definite screw loose.*

The two disappeared and he slumped into the hard chair. Forget getting her help. Looked like he was back to recruiting Thomas Mann.

THE REST of his day went about as well. Joe was out sick, Caleb was blowing a gasket about a skip trace he'd been tracking for months who had eluded him yet again and Cooper Harris was waiting for Malachi in his office when he arrived at Bondsman Brothers.

The leader of the SCVC Taskforce, known as the Beast, was drinking coffee and texting, his dark hair still wet from a shower. Or possibly a swim. He looked fit, always running and surfing. He'd be a good training partner, if Malachi was one for such a thing. "Sleeping in this morning?" he goaded.

"Don't be throwing shade, man." He bumped fists with him and pulled out his chair, the wheels squeaking. "What's up?"

The big man pocketed his phone, looking uncomfortable in the too-small chair. Malachi liked that piece of furniture. Most people found it hard as a rock and the dimensions were wrong for the average person's derriere. Made them leave quickly. "I come asking for a favor. It involves an assignment you worked last year."

Malachi took his seat, wishing he'd snagged another energy drink on the way in. He could tell he was low on electrolytes. He'd have to ask Josie to run to the corner convenience mart and find some sustenance for him on her lunch hour. It would cost him, but he didn't have time to leave again. As executive officer of BB, he had a shit ton of work to do. "Go on."

Harris tucked away his cell and leaned back. "We believe Newt Marcher is returning to the States to resurrect the Quattro Gang. His father's lieutenants are making a run against him."

Fuckers. Jamarion King and Leandro Lopez had done Damon Marcher's bidding and kidnapped the mayor's sister over a year ago. Lopez had been the single fugitive Malachi had searched for and never captured. If he had... "You guys nailed King, along with Damon. Sure wish you'd gotten Lopez, too."

"And now Damon's dead, but Newt is still out there, along with Lopez. We hope to nab both, using King."

A flash of memory tugged at Mal's brain, then vanished. "But King's in prison."

"He cut a deal with the Bureau to give us Newt. This is all hush-hush, mind you. The FBI doesn't want the public to know he's out on the streets, but he's the bait they need to capture Newt. Newt is the big fish they want, and if they nab him, there's far less chance for the QC to be resurrected. Meanwhile, word is King has already recruited Leandro Lopez to join him."

"The gang's all here." Malachi slammed a fist on his desk. Lopez had earned a place in hell, if Mal had any say in it. Maybe, just maybe, if he'd captured the guy, Lopez wouldn't have served up Mia Livingston to Marcher. "If Lopez is back, I *will* catch him."

"That's why I'm here. Dupé prefers that you not."

"Fuck that."

Harris crossed an ankle over his knee. "I know how you feel. My boss would be here himself asking for your cooperation, but I volunteered to speak with you because of our relationship. We're keeping this knowledge on the down low for the next forty-eight hours. That's all we need. Hopefully," he added. "Dupé and the Justice Department have given King that much time to draw Newt out and give them evidence to get the bastard life in prison. It's not much time, and a lot is riding on this. If we get Newt, you'll get Lopez."

Malachi drummed his fingers on the desktop. The West Coast Director of the FBI *should* be here, not Harris, with this Godzilla of a request. "Does the mayor know about this sting operation?"

Harris nodded. "She wants all of those responsible for her sister's ordeal brought to justice, and now that Damon is out of the picture, this is her opportunity to make sure King and Lopez pay for their crimes, too. Bonus, we stop Newt from resurrecting the QG."

"How much of King's sentence did the Feds take off?"

"Nothing, unless he brings us Newt and the proof we need to put him away. If he does that, and they can charge the kid as an accessory for Mia, he gets his sentence reduced from life to thirty years."

"Thirty?" Malachi rocked back and ran a hand through his hair. "He deserves the chair."

"You and I will be old men by the time he's out, if he even makes it that long."

Perspective. He was usually the one preaching it to his siblings. "Speak for yourself on the old man thing."

"You're looking pretty lean. You running again?"

Harris himself was a runner and loved to surf as well.

Malachi tapped a paper calendar on the wall behind him. It was from the local shelter and had a different dog or cat each month. "I'm doing the marathon in January."

"Good for you. I thought about attempting the half next month, but having a family cuts way down on my workout time."

Even the Beast had settled into family life. He had a dog, too. "Tough problem to have." Mal rocked his chair again, his thoughts jumping in all directions. Two days wasn't long to sit on his hands, and he had plenty to keep him occupied, but the thought of Jam King and Leo Lopez running free and partnering up once more made his guts twist. Who knew what kind of hell they could rain down on innocent people? "What if they go after Mia again?"

The Beast untangled his legs and sat forward. "Why would they? It was Damon who had a hard-on for manipulating the mayor. I doubt Newt cares about her and her policies one way or the other."

Still didn't sit well with him. "Dupé's putting extra protection on them both, right?"

"The Marshals are handling it, but Amber doesn't want Mia to suspect anything, so it's all covert."

Malachi stood and held out his hand. It was against his better judgment to agree with this plan, but he was just a lowly fugitive apprehension agent, not a big wig government one. "Forty-eight hours. If you need my help..."

Harris shoved himself to standing and shook on it. "I know where to find you."

The whole thing kept Malachi stewing the rest of the day. He went for another run after work, but not even pushing his body to the breaking point kept his anger at Lopez and the others at bay.

So he forced himself to go to a support meeting at the

church downtown, hoping peer intervention might take his mind off the fact he'd agreed to do nothing while this was all going down.

He was ten minutes late when he slipped into the back row and took the only available seat. A man was at the podium, talking about his fear of the desert after nearly dying during a mission in Sudan.

A soft whine made Malachi glance down. Dark eyes stared up at him from the floor. He smiled at Ladybug, shocked and amused, and the body next to him stiffened. He turned to her owner. "We meet again," he said under his breath.

A faint wave of panic crossed her face. "You," she whispered.

Jokingly, he pointed at the cheap metal seat under him. "Is this yours?"

It was the wrong thing to ask. She jumped up, tugged on the dog's leash, and ran for the door.

THREE

"Hey, wait," McHottie called, his deep baritone echoing on the street.

Mia kept walking, her gait brisk and adrenaline pumping hard.

"I didn't mean it." She heard his footsteps as he ran to catch up to her. "Don't go."

Darkness had fallen and the roads were damp with rain. The brief shower was already done, leaving the sidewalk slick and abandoned in its wake.

She had no car, no ride, and nowhere safe to go. Ladybug kept the pace she set as she fumbled with her phone. "Leave me alone."

Under a light, he fell into stride with her, the scent of clean soap filling her nose as if he'd just stepped out of a shower. "Please don't go because of me. I was joking. I didn't mean to upset you."

He was taller than she'd anticipated. Her pulse kicked when she glanced up at his face, her finger hovering over the number for a ride. Sue would be off at this time of night, but someone else would be available. "I don't know who you are, but you need to back off."

Ladybug wagged her tail as he slowly raised his hands in the air in a surrender gesture and did indeed step back. "Name's Malachi, and I mean no harm. I'll leave if you want."

The shadows were thick around them and she didn't like standing under the glow of the solar light. Taking her own step away from his intense size and muscles, she eased into the murkiness of the building's shade. "Why?"

"Because obviously, you're here for a reason. You need a support meeting."

"And why are you here?"

He lowered his hands and glanced down at the sidewalk. "Because I do as well."

She didn't want to believe him. Didn't want to trust that it was coincidence he'd turned up this morning and again now, in her space.

No such thing as coincidence. Her kidnapping had taught her that. A nice guy, handsome, shows up out of the blue and starts chatting you up? Run the other direction. If not, you could end up in the trunk of his car, in a bare room, screaming for your life. "You expect me to buy the idea that you're not following me? That you just happened to be at the library in my spot this morning, and now you're here?"

Dark eyes met hers once more. "I'm not, I swear. I don't even know you." He seemed to hesitate. "I don't think, anyway. You seem vaguely familiar. Must be the dog."

He gave her a lopsided, hopeful grin.

She didn't reciprocate. He'd no doubt seen her on the news after what happened, her photo on every newspaper, magazine, and website. Disguises only hid so much. "Look, whoever you are, I just want to be left alone. Please."

The smile fell off his face. "I didn't mean to scare you. I'll find another meeting."

There was something so genuine in his voice, and he seemed so disturbed that she feared him, it made her hesitate. As he began to walk away, she realized she wasn't freaking out—not panic-attack level, anyway. Same as that morning, she was unnerved, but her internal radar wasn't going off.

"Wait." She stepped from the building's shadow. "Why do you need a meeting?"

He slowed and turned to face her. "Got some bad news earlier, and it was accompanied by the fact I can't control what's going on in regard to it."

She knew that feeling. "Bad news sucks."

He nodded and pivoted to leave.

"I have control issues, too," she called. "Which is why I have social anxiety. Logically, I know I can't govern people and situations, but because I can't, I freak out sometimes. Which leads to even less control and patronizing sympathy from those around me."

Ladybug leaned into her leg, full of support. Mia's pulse raced and her ears were filled with the sounds of a car passing by. But she wasn't panicking.

This is good. Maybe the old me really is back.

The man stopped, keeping his body pointed away from her. Did he think she might run if he faced her again? "Do the meetings help?"

They weren't Disneyland, but at times, easier than therapy where the spotlight was all on her. "Sometimes. I haven't been to one in a while."

He glanced over his shoulder. "Did you also get bad news?"

She chuckled without an ounce of humor. "I should consider it good, actually."

His massive body turned slowly, and he stuffed his hands in

his pockets, looking slightly confused. She couldn't blame him, she was, too.

Keeping her phone in hand, she glanced around. A few folks were venturing out again, now that the rain had stopped. There were more cars roaming the area. It wasn't a nasty neighborhood, just tired, she thought.

Know that feeling. "I should be happy. Pumped up, really," she explained. Why wasn't she? "Instead, a part of me wants to go on hiding, stay safe."

"Not journey out into the world," he added.

It was said so softly, she wondered if he'd intended for her to hear. "Yes, that. It's a crutch, according to my therapist."

"We all need a few of those." He continued to keep his distance. "A buddy of mine has walled himself off from mostly everything. He was a Marine, like me, and used to be unstoppable." Malachi smiled, as if remembering better days. "After some shit went down in Chad, though, he was never the same. Has nightmares and a load of social anxiety."

So he understood. At least a little.

Wait. Am I actually having this conversation?

She forced herself to breathe in through her nose and out through her mouth. Her skepticism had reached an all-time high, but this was still too surreal.

He could be lying. Leading her on. Creating some kind of false security.

But why?

She ran a hand over her face. God, she was still so paranoid.

No one is after you anymore. You don't need to worry about being kidnapped, she heard her therapist cajole. That voice morphed into Amber's, the two of them a chorus in her head.

In spite of her attempts to rationalize the situation, the piece of her that still hadn't recovered, wasn't on board. Not yet. She reached in her bag for her stun gun. The cool metal and plastic gave her back some control. "Marines, huh?"

He nodded and looked casual, but she saw how he watched for her hand, now inside the messenger bag. "My twin brother and I joined up and served our country. He was caught in a bad situation, lost some good friends and nearly his life. Scared the shit out of me. We both left after that. He's carrying more baggage than I am, but he lets off steam on a frequent basis. I tend to keep it bottled up."

Going back inside wouldn't hurt. There was a room full of people, and she'd be safe. Standing out here, in the open with him, wasn't.

She released the weapon and removed her hand. "You don't have to leave." She adjusted her grips on Ladybug's leash and the phone, and started for the church entrance. He could either follow or go on his merry way. "Sounds like we both need this tonight."

The vestibule was bright and welcoming and she breathed a sigh of relief being back inside its hallowed walls. A heartbeat later, the man entered behind her, the soft *snick* of the door alerting her.

She tried to keep the smile off her lips, but simply averted her face so he didn't see it. Why did she feel better that he'd returned?

"I didn't get your name," he said as he followed her down the hall to the classroom used for the meeting.

He didn't invade her space, which was nice. The passage wasn't exactly narrow, but he filled it anyway. "I didn't offer it."

He fell silent and nodded, then replied, "Fair enough."

They reentered the room and drew a few looks. The previous speaker had given the podium over to a woman at the platform. She paused in her story, allowing them to take their seats before continuing.

Sitting next to Malachi felt comfortable. The room was warm and a bit stuffy, but Mia allowed herself to relax over the next half hour. Neither of them volunteered to share their reason for coming, and after the others finished their stories, the crowd lingered, milling around. Most headed for the table with coffee and store-bought cookies.

Mia avoided Malachi's eyes as she texted her sister. She'd barely listened to the volunteers talking about their problems, or Father Delacroix praying over them, her mind going back and forth on whether or not to tell him her name.

She could give him her fake identity, the one she'd lived under for the past seventeen months, but something about that didn't feel right either. Could she trust him with her real name? *Look at me, making all these positive strides.* The name thing might be too much though.

"Coffee?" he offered, facing the rear of the room where the snacks were set up and indicating the selection.

"God, no. That stuff will rot your insides. The cookies aren't bad, though."

"There's a coffee shop two blocks over."

He looked so hopeful, she felt guilty for turning him down. Staring up into his pretty blue eyes, all that dark hair around his face, made her want to run her fingers through it. "I have another commitment."

"Oh, sure. No problem." He moved to the end of the row, appearing awkward. "Maybe another time."

Amber texted back, letting Mia know she was a block down from the church, as planned.

Ladybug trailed after Malachi and he gave her a parting pet. "It was nice meeting you. Again."

He started for the door and Mia's heart flip-flopped. She couldn't decide whether to rush after him or let him go.

Let him go, her heart warned. *You aren't ready for this.*

Would she ever be? How did you tell even a casual coffee date that you were a whacked out mess? When was the right moment to say, "Oh, hey, by the way, I'm the mayor's sister who was abducted, and I'm living under an assumed identity, scared of my own shadow, these days"?

And that was if he didn't figure it out before she had the chance to come clean. Malachi already believed she seemed familiar.

It was easier to let him go. Smarter, too.

Better for both of them.

Wasn't it?

She stared after him as he slipped out and the door shut.

Ladybug whimpered and Mia bit her bottom lip.

Stupid. What harm would it do to give him her name? Just her first would do. Plenty of folks who attended these meetings kept their full identities a secret.

But now he was gone.

Malachi.

How many guys with that name lived in the city?

Rising from her chair, she hoisted the messenger bag onto her shoulder. *Let him go,* her brain chanted.

Besides, if he *was* who he claimed, he deserved better than her.

And if he was some leftover from the Quattro Gang...

She reached for the stun gun, worrying it a bit inside the bag. Damon was gone and it was time to live again, like Amber said. Mia had to stop fearing every shadow, every...

Coincidence.

The word rankled, no matter how she examined it. Her nerves felt too sensitive, clawed by the idea that she might be duped again.

Ladybug pawed at her shin. "It's fate," her mom had told

her after the ordeal when Ladybug had crawled into her lap in the hospital room. "She'll help you, just like she did Millicent."

Mili. Their younger sister, diagnosed with a rare form of leukemia at sixteen years old. Ladybug had been her therapy dog. Five years after Mili's death, the animal was now Mia's.

Fate. Was there such a thing?

Ladybug tugged her toward the door.

FOUR

Malachi told himself it was no big deal that she hadn't told him her name as he ambled down the damp sidewalk toward the parking garage. If he did some digging, he could find out what it was. Father Delacroix probably knew it, and the librarians.

Hell, Joe, the Cahill brother with the hacking skills, could get into the library's system and find it and her number in thirty seconds flat.

But that wasn't fair, and downright stalker-ish. She'd obviously survived a trauma and felt uncomfortable giving a stranger her information. He respected that and would in no way undermine her wishes.

Damn, that smile, though. A ghost of one, anyway, that had lit up her face, her eyes. She'd attempted to hide it, and it had made him want to see it again, to do whatever it took to turn that light on and give her the courage to show it to him.

He crossed the alley to the next block. A nice, but conservative limo was parked at the curb. Three blocks down the steep hill, the traffic lights flipped from green to yellow, two cars coming to a stop. Their taillights flickered in the puddles on the wet road.

A lone, black SUV drove past. The overhead streetlight's glow rolled over its windshield, the vehicle driving so slowly, it made his hackles rise. Whoever was inside was looking for something.

Or someone.

This part of town wasn't without its criminal element. Street workers and drug dealers tended to hang in the shadows and alleys a few blocks over, but some bled onto this thoroughfare.

Voices echoed behind him and he glanced back to see several of the meeting attendees spilling out of the bedraggled church and conversing nearby.

He slowed and scanned those exiting for Ladybug and her owner. He didn't immediately see them, but then...the woman was carrying the dog. Their eyes locked across the expanse and she smiled.

Malachi came to a dead stop, turning fully to watch her. Even this far from her, the way it transformed her face made his pulse skip. He lifted a hand in acknowledgment, and she did as well, striding confidently toward him.

His breath seemed to stop in his chest as he watched her maneuver around those loitering on the sidewalk. She hopped over a puddle in the alley entrance. The cigar shop he stood in front of had matching security lights in their two display windows, and the beams cast a soft glow onto her face as she and the dog caught up to him.

"I'll be at the library again tomorrow morning," she said. "If you need help with your homework, or you know, just want to hang out."

His day was booked, but hell if he wouldn't rearrange all of it to meet her. "Same time?"

She nodded and skirted past him, heading for the limo. "From the look of my current assignment," she called back, "I'll probably be there all week."

From the corner of his eye, he registered the same vehicle driving by again. Or was this a different one? Black SUVs were a dime a dozen in this town, limos as well. He rotated to keep her in his sights. "I'll be there."

She glanced down, shy-like, smiling even broader. "Good."

The chauffeur came around to open the door for her. "Evening, miss."

She spoke to him and waved at Malachi, tucking herself and the dog into the backseat, as she called, "See you tomorrow."

With the closing door, she disappeared. He waved back, plenty of ideas about who she was now whizzing through his brain. They pulled into traffic.

The lights at the bottom of the hill had gone through their cycle and were now green again, multiple cars and a bus waiting on the side streets.

She seemed familiar because she was. Plenty of actors, singers, and other well-known folks blew through San Diego on a regular basis. The city had its own fair share of the rich and famous, not to mention wealthy tourists and investors who liked the weather and the ocean. Not many of them had a limo waiting when leaving a peer support group meeting, though.

Less than two percent of the population had green eyes. Natural redheads were uncommon, too. He couldn't identify her yet, but he would, betting money that the hair color wasn't natural, and the green of her eyes was thanks to contacts. Dozens of faces flicked through his brain...no, she wasn't any of those.

Shoving his hands in his pockets, he watched them cruise down the hill. Tomorrow, he'd get her name.

When two black SUVs pulled smoothly from a side street, his hackles rose again. They had to be security, he told himself, as they fell in behind the limo. *That's why they were circling the block—they were waiting for her.*

Maybe she wasn't a famous person, maybe it was her father or mother. That would make sense, and yet…

After his training, and experiences in the Marines, he had a fine-tuned danger meter. Like a hair-trigger, it often went off when least expected, and unwanted. He'd become hyperaware of everything in his environment, and overly suspicious of other people's motives.

While Caleb tended to have a hair-trigger, too, his overreactions brought out his fists. Malachi's made his protective instincts go Code Red.

He was running down the hill before he could second guess himself.

"It's an overreaction," his therapist had told him. "Feeling as though any situation is more hazardous or risky than it actually is. You don't have to throw yourself on every bomb to save those around you, Malachi. And not every stressful or unknown situation is one."

The words rang in his ears as he saw the light switch from yellow to red. The limo came to a stop, an SUV drawing up beside it, the other behind.

They're just bodyguards. He chanted it with every step he took. His body refused to listen, the hair on the back of his neck standing rigid. His gut joined in, cramping hard when he saw the back passenger door of the one on the side open.

A man emerged, dressed all in black with a yellow patch on the arm of his left sleeve. He wore a knitted ski mask and was carting an MP7 submachine gun.

Malachi was closing in. He heard a sudden scream from inside the limo. His blood turned to ice. The brake lights flickered and then the driver must have floored it, sending the vehicle into the oncoming traffic.

Horns blared, the limo clipped the tail of another car. The masked man fired.

Malachi damned himself for not bringing his pistol, but it was frowned upon at meetings. "Stop!" The word burst from his lungs.

No one paid any attention, the few people on the street watching the action at the intersection. The limo rammed a compact car aside and began to accelerate. More horns blared.

Malachi shouted again, hoping to draw the gunman's focus, but the guy was homed in on the limo.

Several other men, all dressed the same, exited the two vehicles. One marched into the intersection and shot out a back tire on the escaping limo. It careened into a parked minivan half a block farther down.

Both SUVs zoomed toward it, wheeling around the stopped traffic and edging up to the stalled vehicle, boxing it in. Malachi sprinted past two trucks, jumped over the hood of a car, and shouted again at the top of his lungs, "Stop, you fucking bastards!"

One of them actually flicked a glance at him before descending on the limo with his pals. A shot to the handle disabled the lock. He jerked the door open.

The driver bailed, blood gushing down his nose from meeting the steering wheel. He raised a handgun, but before he could fire, he was hit in the temple with the butt of his weapon. The attacker said something in another language and laughed when the big guy dropped like the two-hundred pound weight that he was to the ground.

It was three against one. There were also two still in the

SUVs, driving. Malachi knew those odds sucked, but as he saw a woman being dragged from the backseat by her hair, he didn't care.

Not Ladybug's owner. Another woman, dressed in a red power suit and swearing her ass off as the gunman used a hunk of tresses to force her toward a waiting vehicle. She kicked and swung at the guy, managing to grab the mask of the one they were passing and yanking it up over his chin. Ladybug barked and her owner screamed from inside the interior. "Amber!"

The half-masked bastard pointed his semiautomatic into the limo at her.

"Noooo!" Malachi hit the intersection at a dead run. Several people had climbed out of their cars, befuddled, and examining the damage. Others stayed inside away from the men with the weapons. "Leave her alone!"

The dog launched herself at the man and got hit for her trouble, landing on the ground in a whimpering heap. A whistle from the leader brought the guy's head around. He said something, again in a language Malachi didn't understand. The accent he knew though—Asian. Half-mask locked eyes with Malachi.

The woman they were kidnapping was unceremoniously shoved into the closest ride as Malachi covered the last few steps. The lone attacker on the street watched him, a grin splitting his acne scarred face still on view. Malachi balled a fist, ready to strike, when Ladybug's owner scrabbled from the damaged vehicle, falling out of the leather seat and screaming for the dog.

The man moved, avoiding Malachi's tackle and kicking her instead. Malachi managed to get a hand on his bulletproof vest, but the asshole spun from his grip. The stock of the gun knocked Malachi in the kidney.

He felt nothing but rage, spinning and reaching for the

bastard again, but the woman clawed at his leg and begged him to save her sister.

"I shoot her, huh?" The man said with a sneer as he waved the end of the weapon at Ladybug's owner. He backed toward the SUVs gunning their engines, and winked at her. "I'll come back for you."

Malachi moved to block his view of her and the dog, raising his hands. "Leave her be."

The guy snickered. "Maybe I'll shoot you instead."

Malachi was pretty sure it was his last breath, but then a passenger door opened and the gunman was ordered by another accented male voice. "Get in!"

"Next time," the guy told Malachi and winked again, sliding the knitted material back over his chin.

Then the SUVs drove away, tires squealing as they went.

"No!" the woman screamed, reaching toward their departing taillights from her spot on the wet pavement. She sat on the road at Malachi's feet, hugging the injured dog to her chest. "Amber!"

Bending down, he was relieved to see she appeared unhurt and the animal was still alive. Ladybug wiggled a bit in her arms and licked her face.

He dialed nine-one-one and huddled over her. "I'll get her back," he whispered into her hair. "I promise."

She raised her tear-soaked eyes to his, gasping for breath. "Mia." She held out a shaking hand to him. "My name is...Mia."

Everything clicked into place. He knew exactly who she was and what had just happened.

The dispatch operator came on the line. "The mayor has been kidnapped," he told her, reeling off the address and descriptions of the vehicles. "And her sister is in need of an ambulance."

"No." Mia shook her head, wiping at her tears. Ladybug whined and continued to try and alleviate her panic. "We have to...We have to go after them." Her gaze trailed in the direction the vehicles went. "And we have to do it now."

FIVE

I *will not panic.* Amber was depending on her.

But the police were in her face, and Ladybug was hurt and limping, and Malachi was several yards away, arguing with a detective.

Mia's breath felt stuck in her ribcage. Her feet weighed a hundred pounds each. She wanted to melt into the night and disappear.

Her mother's crying and her father's raging during her call to tell them what had happened had nearly done her in. The two of them were in San Francisco, on a quick anniversary getaway. They'd never expected Mia to interrupt this special time and tell them such awful news.

They were getting on the first flight available, but it would be morning before they arrived. She couldn't be a coward tonight. No, she had to push past the fear and desperation. Be logical, determined, confident.

In other words, be the woman she *used* to be.

The *warrior* she used to be.

Damn, she hated being so fragile. So unable to control her stupid emotions!

"So, there were three of them," the cop stated, looking back over his notes.

"Plus the drivers." She rubbed a shaking hand over her face, kept her gaze on Ladybug. *I will control my breathing.*

"And they wore masks?"

"I've answered that question twice already." She came to her feet, shoving out of the seat of the police car. "I need to speak to Malachi."

The officer chewed a big wad of gum and smacked it. "Not while he's being interviewed by Detective Eastman."

She glared at him. "You're wasting my time and his. My sister—the *mayor*—has been kidnapped! While you're stand there treating us like criminals, the real ones have gotten away!"

"Now, ma'am, calm down."

"*Ma'am?*" Her voice came out high and incredulous. Ladybug whined and Mia adjusted her hold, desperate not to cause the poor dog more pain. Her bag strap slid down her arm and she hoisted it back up, frustrated. "Did you just ma'am me?"

He had the good sense to step back. "The FBI has been alerted, and we're doing everything we can to find the abductors."

She shoved past him and marched toward Malachi. She didn't have a car, the limo was being towed, and she needed a ride. First to get Ladybug checked out at the closest vet, and then to find Amber.

"Wait, you can't—"

When the cop reached for her arm, she wheeled around and raised a fist. "Don't even think about touching me. I'm done answering questions."

The gum smacking ceased and he cocked a brow at her. He

started to say something, apologize maybe, but she pivoted and started walking again.

Her ribcage actually loosened a notch when she saw Malachi's broad shoulders and firm stance. He'd saved her and her dog. She sucked in the cool night air. "Hang in there, Ladybug," she murmured, transferring the strap so it crossed her body. "We're going to get you looked at in a minute."

Malachi turned, as if sensing her approach, his face thunderous. "Are you all right?"

No, she wasn't. "We need to go. Now."

Detective Eastman studied her, brown furry brows drawing tighter than they'd been with Malachi. "You've been through a traumatic event," he stated with hollow sounding empathy. "I understand you're upset, but I need to be sure we have your statements thoroughly documented. Even the smallest detail may help us find your sister, Ms. Livingston."

"My dog is injured." She grabbed Malachi's hand and tugged him away. "I'm taking her to the all-night emergency care veterinarian. If you have follow-up questions, you have my number."

Malachi didn't resist and neither of them responded when the detective tried to verbally exert his right as a cop to stop them. "Cahill, we need to talk," he insisted.

"Tomorrow," Malachi replied over his shoulder. "Go find the mayor."

The detective jogged to catch up as they passed by the officer who'd been interviewing her. Wiser than his superior, he simply stepped out of the way.

"I'm sorry about what happened," Eastman said to Mia.

She kept going.

"Hold on. This is a serious matter." He stepped in front of her.

Tendrils of surrender wound around her ribcage. Up until

her ordeal, she'd usually had no issues deferring to those in authority. Now? She gritted her teeth and battled those tendrils, facing the detective with absolute wrath. "You don't think I know that? I was taken by that gang seventeen months ago. Do you know what they did to me? Of course, you do. Everyone in the country knows, because it was national news. I almost died because of them, and now they've taken her. *My sister.* They didn't have mercy for me, and they won't have any for her, so get the hell out of my way, and don't ever think you can school me about the seriousness of this situation."

Her chest rose and fell rapidly. She started marching again, doing her best to control her breathing. It was like dragon fire and her vision blurred with anger.

When Eastman shouted, "You don't know it's the same gang," she flipped him the bird over her shoulder.

Malachi fell into step beside her. "My car is in the parking garage. I'll take you anywhere you want to go."

Tears sprang to her eyes at the kindness. No questions asked, no harping over her well-being or state of mind. Focused on the next step, the anger channeled into a more productive energy. They were moving, doing something. "I like a man of action."

He chuckled without a trace of humor. "I hate sitting on my hands."

The street was nearly deserted, the damaged cars gone. Rusty, the limo driver, was at the hospital. The EMT had assured her he would be okay, but would need to undergo a seven day concussion protocol. "I can't believe the police resisted getting on their trail immediately."

His long legs had no trouble keeping up with her pace, although she was practically jogging. "Even if you and I had lit out right behind them, it's doubtful *we* could have tracked them. Those guys are professionals. You're sure it's the Quattro Gang?"

Her throat went tight, like she'd swallowed a pill and it was stuck in her larynx. She hugged Ladybug and swallowed past it. "The man who was going to shoot us? I recognize his voice. He was part of the team that took me that night—when I was kidnapped."

Malachi's step slowed. "Leandro Lopez? That wasn't him."

"I don't know his name." Her stomach was sure, though. Every time she remembered that night, she heard that cold, merciless voice. "I never saw his face, thanks to the hood one of the others rammed over my head, but that accent? Yeah, he was part of the team."

"Damn it. I should have stopped him," Malachi said.

They passed a row of closed shops. Sirens echoed on the wind in the distance. Another accident, or crime, the cops needed to respond to. "How? You did what you could."

"Story of my life. Too bad it's never enough."

She felt his pain, his anger over it. "I know that feeling, but we can't focus on what we should have done." Her therapist was pouring out of her mouth now. Usually, she mentally rolled her eyes at this speech, but it gave her an anchor under the current situation. "You stepped in front of a gunman and were willing to take a bullet for me. I can't thank you enough, but we have to focus on what we can do in *this* moment."

The garage was up ahead. He pulled keys from his pocket and they jingled. "You'll have to give me the address for the vet clinic."

He didn't like glory, to be recognized for his bravery. Okay, she could appreciate that.

One step at a time. Mia dropped a kiss on the dog's head. "I will fry the skin from that guy's entire body when I get hold of him," she told her.

Ladybug whimpered and licked her chin.

"She's a trooper," Malachi remarked.

Mia felt her heart pinch. Ladybug *was* a trooper. Her whole family was. After what they'd all been through...

Amber. The old panic rallied under her skin, threatening to overwhelm her at any second She'd already lost one sister, she wasn't about to lose the other. *Stay focused on logic, not emotion*. That was key.

The garage was dark, lit only by infrequent wall lamps that glowed an off-white. The air was laced with the scent of rubber, oil, and gas. Following him to the second floor, he stopped at a fancy truck and the brake lights flickered when he hit the key fob. "We'll take care of her first, then get more feet on the street to find your sister."

An idea struck as he helped them up into the high seat. "Are you some kind of cop?"

His mouth tweaked. "No, I'm not in law enforcement, but I have a working knowledge of it."

Whatever *that* meant. She eyed him. Through the years, she'd brushed elbows with types like him, thanks to Amber's involvement in government. "Let me guess, you're a spy or with some other alphabet agency that you can't tell me about."

That brought a laugh. He got in and the engine roared to life. "Not hardly. I'm a fugitive apprehension agent."

"A bounty hunter?" Her mouth hung open. *That* she had not expected. She adjusted her messenger bag. "Like that Dog guy on TV?"

Another chuckle as he backed out of the parking spot and headed for the gate. "Not quite, but there are similarities. I run Bondsman Brothers Agency and we specialize."

Again with the vagueness, but she liked seeing him smile. "In what?"

He stopped at the ticket booth and paid. "We work with certain arms of the government on high-risk cases."

Somewhere in there was the truth. She punched the address of the vet into his on-dash GPS. The female voice of the nav system purred, instructing him to turn left as they entered the street. "So you hunt spies and other fugitives who've been trained by our government when they go to the dark side?"

Surprise animated his features, his face spotlighted by the equally spaced street lamps. "In a nutshell, yes."

For some reason, she felt as though she'd just gotten a gold star. "Do you get hazardous pay?"

The smile dimmed. "I wish. We're lucky to keep our business in the black."

The street lights sent waves of ghostly bars across the hood and into her lap. Ladybug kept holding up her paw. She was trembling now and Mia's heart squeezed. "There must be some excellent benefits, at least."

He seemed to think this over. "My brothers and I get to use our training and we work side-by-side with good people. Not everyone has a job like that."

The nav voice spoke again, and Mia fell silent. She couldn't stop hearing Amber yelling, couldn't stop seeing the eyes of the man who'd hurt Ladybug. *I'll come back for you.*

She rubbed a hand over her face. After her rehab stint, she'd taken self-defense classes, including weapons training. She'd even considered carrying a handgun initially, but it never felt right. Instead, she always had her pepper spray and stun gun. Neither had helped her tonight, both buried in the bottom of her bag. *I'll be waiting,* she mentally told her attacker.

As if he knew where her thoughts had gone, Malachi reached over and gently touched her arm. "There was nothing you could have done."

It sounded good, meant to pacify her, soothe her aching heart. She could tell by his tone, he believed it. She'd basically told him the same thing only minutes ago.

He certainly had more insight and experience with the world of criminals, but the scene played over and over. There had to have been something—*anything*—that she could have done differently. "Why did they take her?"

"You're sure it's the same group?"

She nodded.

"The FBI will expect a ransom demand. They'll want you under their watch to take the call when it comes."

"No one has my number except Amber and our parents. I've been...hiding for a while. It's more likely the bastards will call Mom and Dad if they want money, but..." She didn't think that was the odds-on probability. "This isn't a normal kidnapping. This is revenge."

They drew up in front of the clinic, a smattering of lights on inside and no other cars out front. Malachi shifted into park. "Why do you think that?"

One of the two light fixtures over the entrance was burned out. That's how she felt—like part of a pair, but her other half now missing. "Any kind of interaction, like receiving a ransom payment, creates a trail, makes them vulnerable." During her own situation, she'd overheard Damon discussing it with another man. "Since Amber is mayor, the FBI—along with every law enforcement group in the area—will go all out to hunt them down and prosecute. They'll have to be extremely careful, and one of them was already sloppy and nearly had his mask yanked off by my sister. They want her for something besides money, and I'm afraid her time is running out."

Malachi exited and came around to help her and Ladybug down. "If they'd wanted to kill her, they would have done it publicly in the street. She's alive, you can bet on it, and that means we've got a chance."

"I want to believe that," she admitted, following him to the entrance. "I really do."

He pinned her with a look before he opened the glass door. "Your sister never gave up hope when you were kidnapped. You have to be the one to hold onto that hope this time."

How did he know? Mia sighed and nodded. *I'll try.*

SIX

The plastic chair made his butt hurt, so Malachi stood and paced the waiting room. Old flyers, faded and worn, hung on a bulletin board advertising dog-sitting services, a free spay clinic, and a few missing pets.

Mia and Ladybug had been in the back with the on-call veterinarian for nearly an hour. There was only one technician on duty, who was also in the room down the hall, and nobody at the desk. The phone rang every few minutes, but each call seemed to go to voicemail after two rings. The place wasn't totally rundown, but it had certainly seen its share of drudgery, and it smelled of wet dog.

He texted Caleb, instructing him to round up the troops and meet him at the office. Within minutes, he received several threatening responses until he explained it had to do with the kidnapped mayor and her younger sister.

A small box TV from another century played in the corner. The news was on every channel about the abduction. A woman in the crowd had caught parts of the scene on her smartphone and it was now on all social media outlets as well. Growling under his breath, he watched himself step in front of Mia and the dog, willing to take a bullet for them. He fired off a message to Harris, informing him that it was possible Jamarion King was behind it.

He was pacing for the twentieth time when his cell rang, Harris on the other end. "What the actual fuck happened tonight, and why were you with Mia Livingston?"

"I'll explain later. Right now, Amber is in deep shit, and Dupé better put everyone he's got on her trail."

"If he gets word that I told you about King, Marcher, and Lopez, and the deal the Feds have on the table, he will skin us both alive."

Malachi rubbed his tired eyes. "I won't throw you under the bus, but here's the thing—if King or Newt Marcher have resurrected the gang, this looks like pure revenge. They have nothing to gain by kidnapping the mayor."

"You're confident the culprits tonight are part of the old QG?"

He wasn't. Mia was. For now, that was good enough for him. "I couldn't ID any of them in a lineup, if that's what you're asking, but what are the odds it's anyone else?"

Harris sighed. "I gotta go. Dupé's calling. Keep in touch, and stay the fuck away from Mia Livingston."

Malachi bit his tongue as the line went dead. That was the last thing he planned to do.

A flyer with a dog's sad face caught his eye. A rescue looking for a home, it had been found as a stray and was in foster care. The pit mix had scars around his face and those sad eyes seemed to have given up on the world. The description confirmed the dog had most likely experienced a hard life up to this point and Malachi felt a bond with the animal. The foster had named him Ollie, but Malachi thought he looked more like a Boomer, or maybe a Ranger.

The door to the back opened and Mia came out with Ladybug in her arms. The dog's leg was wrapped in so many bandages, it stuck straight out. "All done," she said. "Can you grab my bag so I can pay?"

His phone, still in hand, rang. The screen showed Victor Dupé. For a second, he considered answering, then sent it to voicemail. He had better things to do then get his ass chewed by someone who wasn't his boss.

"Is she going to be okay?" The bag was heavy and it surprised him somewhat.

She accepted it and allowed him to carefully relieve her of the dog while the vet tech went behind the desk and tapped keys on the computer. "The leg is badly bruised, and there's a tiny hairline fracture near her shoulder, but nothing is truly broken. I've got some pain meds for her, and the swelling should go down in a few days."

The poor canine stared at Malachi as though she'd been tortured. He scratched behind a floppy ear and smiled into her scruffy face. "You were very brave back there."

His phone rang again, and he didn't bother to look. One guess who it was.

He did wander over to the board and snap a photo of the foster's number, just in case. In case what, he wasn't sure. Yes, a dog would be nice, but did he really have time for one? Could he be a good dog parent when he was gone at all hours, sometimes for days at a time?

Caleb and Josie would watch it for him, but they had several cats. What if Boomer didn't like cats?

Great, I've already named it. That couldn't be good.

Mia finished, a deep crease between her brows as she turned from the counter and returned her wallet to her bag. Vet bills were expensive and Malachi wondered if she needed cash.

Back inside the truck, he assisted with getting Ladybug

situated between them on an old sweatshirt of his. Then he glanced at Mia. "The FBI knows you're with me and they've been calling. Do you want to talk to them?"

She worried her fingers in her lap. "Guess I should. I don't know what I can tell them that I didn't already recount to the police."

"I assume you don't necessarily want them at your place. We can use my office, if you prefer. I'd also like to bring my brothers in on this to help. We're not law enforcement, as I told you, but we have a lot of combined knowledge about this city and the criminals who occupy it."

"Sure." She stifled a yawn. "Whatever I can do to up the odds of finding her, I'm in."

She was going to be a zombie if she didn't get some sleep. He couldn't provide that just yet, but maybe a meal would help. "Have you ever had a breakfast burrito?"

Her brows rose in a question. "Can't say that I have, why?"

Shifting into gear, he grinned. "There's an all-night food truck near the office. Family run operation with the best Mexican this side of the border. The coffee's borderline, so I don't recommend that, but the food is delicious. You're going to love it."

She didn't protest and he drove to the all-night stand. The owner, Yoán, hailed him when Malachi got out, and Mal bought extra for everyone he expected to be at Bondsman Brothers.

He was glad he did. The lights inside the building seemed harsh, probably because he was so tired. Caleb hit him with, "What the fuck?" before the chime over the front door finished its *bing-bong*.

"Everyone, this is Mia." He handed Caleb one bag and Joe the other. Then he made the round of introductions. "Mia, meet Josie, Sam, Caleb, Joe, and Jack-Jack."

Mia cradled Ladybug, who leaned over her arm to sniff as Jack-Jack greeted them. The Jack Russell terrier stared up with curious eyes and offered a bark that Malachi assumed was a hello.

Ladybug lifted her chin and looked away. Jack-Jack seemed confused and Malachi tried not to laugh. The ladies usually loved the former street dog. "Give her some space," he told Jack-Jack. "She'll come around."

The group gave Mia hellos and chin nods, already digging into the extremely early morning breakfast. Josie, the best office manager around, had coffee brewed and a selection of cold drinks available. Each of them grabbed a foil-wrapped burrito and their choice of beverage and headed for the conference room. Jack-Jack followed.

As Mia laid Ladybug, half-wrapped in Malachi's sweatshirt, in the corner, he made a place for her at the table. Jack-Jack lay down not far from the visiting dog, his nose going crazy between sniffing her and the air with the tantalizing scent of food on it. Mia joined them and Malachi sketched out the events of the night, along with what the two of them believed about the abductors.

As everyone asked questions around bites of food, Caleb left and came back with his laptop. "The Quattro Gang doesn't have any leadership. They scattered after Marcher's arrest." He licked two of his fingers, wiped his hands on a napkin, and opened the computer. "I'm sure most were just laying low, but this seems intricate for them to pull off so successfully. You said the guy who spoke to you sounded Russian?"

"Or possibly Eastern European." Malachi downed a swig of coffee. "I'm bad with those accents. The others sounded Chinese, or perhaps Korean." He glanced at Mia. "What do you think? Any idea what nationality he is?"

She swallowed and nodded. "Definitely Eastern European, but not Russian."

Caleb typed. "He had scars on his face?"

Malachi finished off his burrito. "From acne."

Josie leaned over to read Caleb's screen. "You think you can get a hit off that little?"

"I'm adding the Quattro Gang as a parameter. Did any of the others who kidnapped you have accents?" He directed this at Mia.

Malachi saw her purse her lips before she answered. "Not anything distinct, and Marcher only ever allowed a few of his men near me during my ordeal. They moved me around, but didn't speak to me."

"Can you walk us through the night they took you?" Sam asked.

She sat back, frowning. Her gaze stayed glued to the table-top, and Malachi's stomach flip-flopped seeing her obvious distress.

"You don't have to," he told her. "If it's too traumatic."

Sam gave him the hairy eyeball, but stayed quiet, waiting.

"It was a dinner at one of the Bayfront hotels—the Hilton," Mia said quietly. "An organization called She Paints was honoring Amber. They support trauma victims through the arts —painting, sculpture, music, writing—and she's a big advocate for them. A waiter told me there was a man in the lobby who wanted to make a contribution to Amber's reelection campaign, and had asked to speak to me specifically." She glanced up. "A politician can never say no to funding, so I went. Except the guy wasn't in the lobby, he was outside, smoking a cigarette."

"Jam King," Joe supplied.

She nodded. "He apologized for his *nasty habit*, and said he appreciated me meeting with him. He pointed to a limo waiting for him and stated he was on his way out of town for business and wouldn't return for a while. He exclaimed over Amber's achievements, and asked me to walk with him and explain her stand on crimes against women." Again her gaze rose. "Irony there, right? As we talked, he led me toward the limo, saying he wanted to write a check. Once we were there, someone came up behind me, put the hood over my head, and I was shoved into the trunk."

"I'm so sorry," Josie sympathized. It wasn't pity in her eyes or tone, but a woman-to-woman solidarity he thought. "Fucking assholes."

Mia's eyes teared but she blinked them away. "I was too trusting, gullible. I never should have left the event."

"It wasn't your fault," he insisted. "It's not about being trusting or gullible. They targeted you. You're not to blame—they are."

The corner of her lips quivered in a half-hearted smile. "My therapist says the same thing."

No one here knew about the deal the Bureau had made with King and Lopez. Malachi rubbed the back of his neck and grimaced, then spilled what Harris had told him.

Everyone stopped eating and looked at him, then Mia. Mouth open, she slammed her hand on the table, and some of the contents of her burrito went flying. "What the hell?" Her sharp eyes pinned him. "When were you going to tell me this?"

Never. "I wanted to earlier, but our first concern was the dog."

She started to say something else, then closed her lips. Her cheeks grew red, as though she were holding in her anger.

"I'm sorry," Malachi added. "Not only for not informing you sooner, but also the fact that the FBI is playing games with this. You should also know Amber was in on the sting."

Her mouth fell open again. "What? Why?"

"My understanding is that she wants all of those involved brought to justice."

"How could she not tell me?"

He wanted to reach out and take her hand, but thought better of it. She was barely holding it together, and rightly so. "I'm sure she didn't want to worry you."

Her gaze went down and her chest rose and fell in a huge sigh. She squeezed her eyes closed for a moment, then blinked them open, but still didn't look at anyone. From the floor, Ladybug whined.

"Well, that changes everything," Sam said. Drawing out her phone, she texted someone, and he hoped it wasn't Harris. He was her immediate boss now that she'd left her former position with the FBI. "I can't believe the JD cut a deal with that scum."

"It's horrible." Mia pushed her mangled food aside. "They're as much to blame as anyone." Her face was blotched and she glared at Malachi. "I want nothing to do with any of them."

Caleb studied his screen, and swallowed a bite. "Unfortunately, I've got nothing on our acne-scarred non-Russian."

Malachi gave Mia a nod, confirming he understood.

Sam didn't. "The thing is, we have the experts and the resources to locate your sister."

"You're an FBI agent?" Mia huffed when Sam nodded.

"I'm with the SCVC Taskforce, under Director Dupé's authority. I'm not assigned to this case—yet—but I can ask to be."

Malachi stepped in. "She's right. We need to work with the Bureau to gain information that can help us get Amber back."

Mia's eyes narrowed.

He motioned around the table. "This group has the capability to get the job done, if we know who and what we're going up against. The only sure way for us to gain those details is if we at least appear to be working with and not against them."

"La, la, la." Sam fake-plugged her ears. "I'm not hearing this."

Mia ignored her. "Well, since the FBI has done little to help me or my sister, I'd prefer to stick with you."

"I'm with Sam." Joe wiped his mouth and swallowed a sip of his drink. "We share everything with the Bureau in good faith. Otherwise, we can get ourselves into some very hot water."

Sam agreed, tucking a wayward lock of hair behind her ear. "We should pool our resources, not scatter them. I'll talk to Coop, come up with a plan for a way the Taskforce can help."

Malachi had finished his burrito and wished he had two more. "Harris told me to stay away from Mia. I don't think he'll suddenly change his mind and want our assistance. The only chance that would happen is if Dupé assigned the Taskforce to the case, and they determined they needed fugitive apprehension agents. Otherwise, why would he do that?"

"Why indeed?" As if they'd conjured him, the West Coast Director of the FBI appeared in the doorway.

"Oh, boy," Caleb quipped. "Do you walk through walls now, too?"

Dupé didn't so much as crack a smile. "The front door was unlocked."

Josie went pale and jumped up. "I'm so sorry," she whispered to the group. "I disengaged it and the chime. I'll go fix that."

As the man moved into the room, Malachi saw Harris behind him. He ran a hand over his face as the two filled the space, both glaring at him.

He motioned at the older man. "Mia Livingston, meet Director Dupé."

He offered a strained smile. "We've been trying to get in touch with you, Ms. Livingston."

She rose and Malachi saw Ladybug try to stand. Her bandaged leg was stiff and she couldn't get her footing. "Have you found her?"

"I'm afraid not, but I'd like to discuss the situation with you. The detective who took your statement mentioned that you're convinced this is the work of the Quattro Gang. While the MO is different, and we don't believe it is them, I'd appreciate you working with my group to review possible places the gang may have held you, in case they give us insight into your sister's whereabouts."

"I never knew the locations. Every time they moved me..." Her voice hitched and Ladybug squirmed again, determined to get to her. Malachi stood, brushing her arm with his in a show of solidarity. She paused, swallowed, and went on. "They kept me blindfolded and drugged."

Dupé's focus flicked to Malachi and back. In that tiniest of movements, Malachi saw the reprimand he was holding in. "Even the most insignificant detail could prove useful. I know you want to do everything possible to end this for your sister."

Her chin rose. "Don't try to manipulate me. I'll go over the details with your agents, but I want Malachi and this team involved every step of the way."

"Technically," Sam said, raising her hand, "I'm the liaison between them. You can talk to me, if that suits."

"As long as Malachi is included," Mia insisted.

The director liked a challenge, as evident in the appraisal he gave her. "We always appreciate the Cahill brothers' expertise, but they aren't qualified for this type of case, Ms. Livingston. Samantha is. I assure you, my Taskforce is the best in the—"

"If you want my help"—Mia's finger punched the table—"it's a package deal."

The corners of Dupé's eyes narrowed. Just a pinch, and then it was gone. He glanced at Harris, who gave a nod, then regarded Mia once more. "Very well. Ms. Livingston, meet Cooper Harris, in charge of the SCVC Taskforce. He and Samantha will review your statements regarding your plight, and forward any helpful information to me. As I mentioned, the Bureau does not believe this is connected to the Quattro Gang, and the kidnappers may reach out with ransom demands. We'd like to have access to your apartment and land-line, as well as your cell, to enable us to trace any calls."

"I don't have a landline, and you can do whatever you want with my cell, but they don't have my number. You're barking up the wrong tree with the idea that they'll contact us with a ransom request, but if they do, it will be to my father and mother."

Dupé gave her that smile again, more patient than stoic this time. "You've thought this through."

Josie returned, exchanging a look with Caleb before returning to her seat.

"Might be wise to listen to her." Malachi gave the director an impassive smile.

"My parents are out of town, but they'll be here in the morning."

A muscle in Dupé's cheek jumped. "As you wish, Ms. Livingston." He withdrew a business card from his breast pocket and handed it to her. "If you need anything or have further insights you'd like to share directly with me, call this number. Otherwise, I'll leave you in the hands of..." He looked around at the group gathered. "These capable agents."

The man left and the room suddenly felt lighter. Harris

rocked on his heels, giving Malachi a stern look. "I warned you not to get involved."

Malachi grinned, just to irritate him further. "Luckily, you're not my boss."

Mia sank into the chair, all the fight gone out of her. She scrubbed her eyes and visibly shook herself. Ladybug whimpered and Malachi picked up the poor dog and placed her in Mia's lap.

She hugged Ladybug gently. "I'm okay," she murmured in her ear. She looked up and met Sam's eyes. "Let's get this over with."

SEVEN

"I'll get you some coffee," Josie said to the man named Cooper. She jumped up once more and rushed out, as if she wanted to get as far from all this as possible.

"Give me a few minutes to access your file." Sam typed on her phone. "I promise to make it as painless as possible."

Malachi stared at her, continually scanning her face and posture. His expression didn't give much away, but Mia could see the worry in his eyes.

She returned Ladybug to the floor, kneeling beside her and petting her soft fur. The vet had removed her vest. She looked smaller and more vulnerable without it.

The other dog, also a terrier, cautiously crawled on his belly toward them, watching Ladybug and sniffing at her thickly bandaged leg. "I can tell you everything I told the agents in two minutes flat." She held out her hand to let Jack-Jack sniff it. "They kept me in cold, humid, nearly soundless rooms. I only ever saw Damon's face— he did the majority of the talking and torture. I heard a few different voices at times, but they blurred together after a while."

Most of Marcher's ranting had been as bad as the physical pain he'd inflicted. He'd said things that made no sense and seemed to suggest he was losing his marbles. "No windows, a weird light behind me, and a chair. That's all I remember."

All eyes were on her. She had to focus on the dogs, feeling her lungs growing tight. The hot sensation of fear climbed into her belly as she blinked away the darkness creeping in. *Breathe.*

Also, do not pass out.

Throat closing up, she shut her eyes and thought of sunflowers and open fields. Blue skies. She counted to four during her inhale, paused, and then eight on the exhale. It forced her nervous system to calm down, a trick her psychiatrist had taught her. Sometimes it actually helped.

Sam started to say something, but her voice cut short. Malachi must have silenced her, giving Mia time to regain her bearings once more. The air felt thick and Jack-Jack pawed at Mia's leg.

Opening her eyes, she found both dogs staring at her. Ladybug leaned against her knee. The thick air filling her lungs lightened a smidge. "I think they moved me three times." She was relieved to hear her voice come out steady and strong. "But every cell looked identical to the last. I'm not sure we actually switched locations, to be honest, although Damon obviously wanted me to believe we had. I think it added to my confusion and hopelessness of being rescued."

A glance at the group confirmed they were all listening closely. Sam was taking notes on a yellow pad. Joe was also writing things down, his movements reminding her of Malachi's. Joe's appearance was similar to the twins, but his hair was a shade lighter, his nose different.

Malachi gave her an encouraging nod. It felt good, bathing her in warmth. Mia found she could give him a faint smile in return.

When Sam glanced up to see Mia waiting, she adjusted her ponytail and read over her notes. "You're doing great," she told her. "When he supposedly moved you, could you tell what type of vehicle you were in? Did you have to climb up into it as if it were a van? Or was it lower to the ground, like a sedan?"

Mia had fought hard to forget all of this—it was like ripping the scab off an old wound. All the memories rushed back, clogging her brain, her throat. The metallic taste of blood, the searing pain from beatings, and thirst...even the slide of the needle under her skin when they drugged her. Those awful memories closed in, causing an icy shiver to cascade down her spine. "They kept me drugged, out of it. Most of the time, I was unconscious, or nearly so, and the trips are a blur. Again, maybe they drove around and came back to the same place, I don't know. Even when I was halfway conscious, I was blindfolded and gagged. It might have been a van, but honestly, I was never conscious enough to get my bearings until we were on the road. I remember one time they sort of rolled me out of a vehicle when we arrived at the next place. Two men picked me up from there and carried me to another cell. That's when I heard the guy with the accent from tonight." The clock on the wall showed it was nearing two a.m. "Last night," she corrected. "That time, I wasn't as out of it as usual. I struggled, trying to get free. It didn't work, obviously, but I gave it all I had."

Her voice shook on the last few words. She could barely look at Malachi.

"They rolled you out?" Joe tapped his pen on his notepad. He glanced at the other's when Mia nodded. "Could they have backed up to a loading dock?"

Caleb typed. "Lots of those in the city. I'll cross-match with places that might have concrete cells."

"Good luck with that," Cooper chimed in. He sat forward, holding Mia's gaze. His was dark, ominous. If he wasn't on their side, she'd be afraid of him. "You said it was cold. Unnaturally so, like they purposely kept it that way? Or was it underground?"

Glances were exchanged. Mia thought about it, but she really had no idea. She gave a shrug. "Sorry."

"There must have been an air vent for circulation," Malachi added. "Did you ever feel cold air coming from it?"

She glanced at the floor, trying to recall those long horrible days without succumbing to them. "Most of the time, I was tied to the chair with my eyes covered." She had to take another slow breath. Ladybug whined, sensing her distress. Being isolated, tortured, and the hope that she'd be found while fearing she never would be had made her half crazy. "I never got a good view behind me, but I did feel cold air coming in. And I think I heard a motor running. The air came from overhead, so that must have been the vent. The only other things I saw were a drain in the floor and the door."

Ladybug scooted even closer, making a soft whimper, using her good leg to paw gently at Mia. She ended up touching Jack-Jack's paw, and the two dogs looked at each other.

Mia glanced at Malachi. A muscle ticked in his jaw. "What about the door?" She could see in his eyes that he hated pushing her, but it was important. "Can you describe it?"

No one had asked her that previously. She closed her eyes and focused on seeing the room again. For Malachi, she could do this. "It had a shiny, sort of reflective glare to it. Pale, like the walls, but it seemed less...hard. Does that make sense? There was a metal handle on it, but of course, it was always locked when no one was in there with me."

Malachi glanced at Cooper. "Insulated?"

The other man nodded. "Marcher was deliberately keeping the place cold. Why?"

"But not freezing," Malachi remarked.

Joe tapped his pen again. "Places like that could include a butcher shop. They have walk-in refrigerators as big as a room."

"From the sounds of it, it was too clean for that," Sam countered. "Florist? They keep buckets of cut flowers in water, so they need a drain, as well as a cooler than room temperature refrigerator."

Mia patted both dogs and stood, stretching her legs. Another memory tickled at her brain but she couldn't catch hold of it, and it passed. "Not a butcher shop. I know that odor."

Malachi shifted in his chair, toying with the wrapper from his breakfast. "What *did* it smell like?"

Besides sweat and blood? Not blood from animals, but her own. "Chemicals." The odor had clung to her nostrils for days after her rescue, no matter how many showers she took or candles she burned.

Sam wrote something down then glanced up at her. "Like cleaning products?"

"Yes and no." Mia was so exhausted yet wired at the same time. Was Amber in one of those cells right now? "I could smell something cloying and kind of weird." She gave them all a desperate look. "Sorry, I don't know exactly what it was, but I hated it. It made me think of death."

There was another quiet exchange around the table. Sam nodded. "Maybe it's a manufacturing plant where they make and use all various chemicals," she suggested to the others.

Josie entered with Cooper's coffee. "I hate to interrupt, but we have a problem."

Malachi's face turned to stone. "What now?"

She motioned at him to follow her. Everyone rose and did the same.

The front of the office contained Josie's desk, a few waiting chairs, and file cabinets. Josie went to the blinds and lifted one of the slats. "You've got fans."

They all seemed to move as one, nearly blocking Mia from looking out with them, but she shoved herself between Malachi and Caleb, both men towering over her.

Joe let out a low whistle between his teeth, and Cooper swore under his breath. Malachi said nothing, but his body was so tense, Mia feared he might punch the window.

Reporters lined the sidewalk and the tiny square of sandy lawn in front of the building. News vans crowded the street, spotlights on cameras cutting across the landscape as several of the bolder reporters knocked on the door yelling questions at Malachi, spotting him through the blinds. Caleb reached around Mia, poking his brother in the shoulder. "The video's gone viral. You're famous, bro."

If possible, he tensed even more. "Fucking A," he cursed, letting the blinds snap back into place. He stepped back and shook his head. "My worst nightmare has come true."

EIGHT

The go signal came at 0220 hours. Thomas checked the readout on his smartwatch, pushed off the wall of the building behind Bondsmen Brothers and kept the brim of his hat down low over his forehead.

The media had packed the area out front, a few stragglers here in the alley on the chance that Malachi Cahill might sneak out the back. The tiny gravel parking lot was filled with vehicles whose owners were inside. Used to undercover work, Thomas knew how to blend in, go unnoticed. Cooper 'The Beast' Harris had anticipated this shit show as soon as the video hit the airways, and as usual, The Beast came prepared.

Thomas toyed with the tiny device in his pocket that would create the diversion they needed once Caleb dashed to Malachi's truck, pretending to be him. While he drew the gawkers and reporters away, Thomas's small and harmless explosive would keep them in chaos, preventing most from following.

Every time he thought about the mayor's kidnapping, her sister's as well, his guts crawled. Unbidden memories of his own encounter with a group of lowlifes who'd tried to get information out of him still wrecked his sleep, haunting his dreams. He didn't know Amber or Mia Livingston, and yet, he wanted to hurt those who had done this.

The combined distractions would give him time to pull the van up to the back and help the real Malachi, and Mia, slip away unnoticed. Keeping his head low, he skirted the crowd and planted the device on the broadcast truck stationed down the street, approximately center of the others. He made sure no one was inside before placing it on the rear cargo doors. He was pleased to see it belonged to one of his least favorite media outlets that consistently searched for the worst stories around and publicized them to keep folks living in fear.

Not that the world wasn't a shitty place. He knew that first-hand from all his Taskforce missions, and those before he'd ended up with Coop. Every day, he hunted the bad guys, hung out with gang members, watched innocent people get hurt. But that's why he did what he did—to try and save those he could.

After he'd secured the device that would simply blow the doors of the truck open and make a deafening noise that led people to believe they were under attack, he jogged to the minivan—classic ride that—and drove it around to the alley.

In position, he typed, sending a text to Coop. *Ready when you are.*

0245 came the reply. Thomas idled, a couple of those staked out eyeballing him. Only a minute until it all went down.

Sure enough, Caleb, pretending to be his brother, drew everyone's attention. Two of the three newshounds left their post and ran for the lot. The other checked his phone.

"Come on," Thomas urged from behind the steering wheel. "Get out of here."

He punched the code into his watch and counted down the seconds.

Boom!

The device sounded like a bomb, then the repetitive tat-tat-tat of gunfire.

There were no guns or bullets. No bombs. But the crowd didn't know that. Screaming ensued, the last asshole watching took off for the street at a run, and Thomas smiled.

At the same time, the back door of Bondsmen Brothers flew open, and he eased the brand new silver minivan—complete with onboard WIFI and third-row seating—as close as he could get to the exit. Coop and Celina had Owen, Nova, and their Chihuahua, Thunder—they hardly needed the extra seats unless, of course, they were planning on adding a few more kiddos to their household.

Good for them. Someday, maybe he and Ronni would start a family, too. If, and only if, he could leave this world behind. Undercover work was in his blood, a way of life. Children needed a father who was home, a nine-to-five job, Little League games, cookouts. Someone to take them to the beach, teach them soccer, buy them ice cream. He wasn't sure he was cut out for that.

Coop emerged first, nodded at Thomas through the windshield, and turned back to hustle the woman, Malachi, Sam, and Joe to the van. Mia Livingston had an oversized sweatshirt on, hood up. Malachi carried a dog with a bandaged leg. Another—Sam and Joe's—dashed out alongside them, barking as if this were a game.

Thomas hit the button to open the side. It slid back noiselessly. Foot runners descended, and a sexy, female-voiced AI explained to him what was happening as if he was an imbecile.

His watch buzzed with another incoming message as the group threw themselves inside.

Target acquired? Ronni wanted to know.

The third-row seat came in handy tonight with the addition of four passengers besides him and Coop, along with the animals. Thomas pressed the yes reply button as Mia sank in behind him. Coop took the passenger seat.

"Bitch'n ride, my man," Thomas smarted off to his boss. "The soccer mom van is definitely stealth material."

The door slid closed, whisper-quiet. Coop glanced back at the others. "Buckle up." To Thomas, he frowned and growled, "Just drive, asshole."

Thomas smiled again, putting the vehicle in gear. "Roger that."

HIS FAVORITE FBI AGENT, Ronni Punto, waited for them at the covert Taskforce office housed in a rundown building across town. Along with a senior center and an accountant, the place was another forgotten commercial zoned building long past its glory days. Thomas smelled the coffee she'd made before they were halfway down the hall.

As he entered, she winked at him from her seat next to Bobby, their computer expert and IT guy, at the far end of the conference table.

No one had said much on the drive over. Caleb had notified Malachi that he'd managed to lead those who did give chase away and lost them. He'd doubled back and picked up Josie. They were staying at the office to make sure no one attempted a break-in. Most of the media crews had cleared out by then, realizing they'd been duped by nothing more than sound effects. "They'll try again tomorrow," Thomas had told Malachi, but for now, everything was quiet there.

Meantime, as Thomas grabbed a cup and sat in a chair, he

covertly studied the mayor's sister. She sat and Malachi placed the injured dog in her lap. Sam filled a bowl with water, offering it to Jack-Jack. Bobby and Ronni introduced themselves, and Coop brought the meeting to order. "Tell them what we've discussed so far," he instructed Sam.

The FBI agent went through her notes, glancing at Mia every once in a while to confirm their accuracy. The woman kept her gaze on the coffee Malachi had set down for her, but her face was determined, if also showing signs of acute exhaustion.

Thomas listened carefully to the descriptions of the holding cells, the rides, the theories the others had come up with. It wasn't nearly enough to start with, but it was all they had.

When the group fell silent, he realized Coop had said something to him. They were all waiting for a response.

The dozens of times he'd been undercover with various gangs, he knew the city inside and out. Knew the dens and headquarters of each. Had visited plenty of the places where they did their dirty work. He knew his comment wouldn't be well received, but on the street, he'd heard plenty of gossip about the Quattro Gang and the way Damon Marcher had operated. He was a legitimate businessman by day and brushed elbows with the thieves, punks, and hitmen he used to eliminate his competition by night. Anyone he didn't like, he tried to blackmail first. If that didn't work? Boom, they disappeared or were found dead.

Marcher had enjoyed a good run, staying out of law enforcement's grasp, but his ego had grown too big. Going after Mia Livingston had been his undoing.

Thomas wasn't the only one who knew how to create a good distraction. "Damon Marcher had a big dick and he liked to swing it around a lot."

Coop cleared his throat, stopping Thomas from going on, and making a quick slashing movement across his neck. What, he couldn't swear in front of Livingston? What kind of bullshit was that?

But he took a deep breath, cleared his throat, and tried to be more polite. Or politically correct. Or something. "He liked to throw his weight around." At Coop's nod, he continued, making a mental note to bust him for it later. "He did a lot of things for show—so everyone knew he was a tough bastard and not one to mess with."

Yeah, he used a colorful term and no one flinched, certainly not Livingston. "Okay, I get it. He had a split identity."

Good, she was quick and smart. Thomas nodded. "He'd send his army of bullies to take out certain gang members he deemed as threats, or anyone he didn't care for. A lot of times it was in showy public ways to send a message to anyone in his territory not to mess with him or his operations. His mercenaries moved fast and they were lethal."

Everyone was looking at him, except Mia, who dropped her gaze.

"What does that have to do with finding the mayor?" Malachi asked grumpily.

Thomas sipped his drink, glancing at Ronni and seeing her small nod. She knew the depth of crime and greed he'd witnessed, the things he'd been through. She was his rock, and the only thing who kept the nightmares at bay. He met Malachi's eyes. "Some of those blatant attacks on his enemies were merely distractions from his other agenda—killing key figures behind the scenes."

Questions dominated the expressions of those gathered. Livingston finally shot a glance his way. "I still don't get what that has to do with my sister."

She might be tired, but she didn't beat around the bush.

Thomas appreciated that. "During Marcher's reign, it's believed he took out scores of players up and down the coast in order to infiltrate their operations. He couldn't go in guns blazing every time, so his second-in-command, Jam King, took to ambushing them and making them disappear. Leo Lopez helped. They left behind no bodies, no evidence, no proof."

Joe leaned in. "How?"

Thomas ran a thumb down the edge of the cup. "It's rumored he had off-the-grid sites for torture and body disposal."

"Disposal?" As realization sank in, Mia's sad, tired eyes filled with horror. She sunk farther in her chair. "You mean, they held me in a...?"

Thomas played with his mug. "Sources on the streets claim Damon Marcher had his own morgue system for storing dead bodies and at least one crematorium for burning them."

NINE

Mia couldn't sit any longer. She stood, shoving back from the table. "Where's the restroom?

Ronni and Sam both jumped to their feet. Ronni put out a hand, signaling Sam to stay. "Follow me. It's right this way."

Malachi took Ladybug from her. With a solemn gaze, he watched as she went out the office door.

Like Sam, Ronni was an FBI agent. She had short dark hair with coppery streaks, her skin was perfect, and her brown eyes missed nothing. She flipped on the hall light, casting a milky glow over them. Mia wished she could step into the shadows along the walls and disappear, but what good would that do Amber? Now that she'd raised those memories, they wouldn't go nicely back behind the mental wall she'd constructed. They filled her head like ping-pong balls bouncing and ricocheting around. Along with them, she also had the imagery Agent Mann had just provided. A crematorium. Super.

Her stomach cramped and released, twisting and plunging, thinking about the fact she'd been held in a place designed exactly to torment, kill, and dispose of her corpse. Amber had to be there, in one of those places.

Jaw tight, she picked up speed, seeing the door marked Ladies. "Thanks," she murmured and jetted for it.

The breakfast burrito came up as she made it to the stall. As images burned into her brain with unbidden abandon, she wretched again and again, her body expelling more than food.

Once her stomach was empty, her belly continued to clench, attempting, but failing, to rid her of the seeping black dread lodged in her bones. The ice filling her veins, the remorse and hate swilling in her blood—it all mixed inside her in a fatal brew.

How long she stayed bent over the porcelain seat, she didn't know. It felt like lifetimes. She grew even weaker, legs trembling. Leaning on the stall's metal partition, she dragged in a tight breath then managed to flush. Feeling as though she had purged herself of more than her breakfast, she released all the pent up anxiety of months living in fear since she'd been rescued, always anticipating the bogeyman might still be waiting for her around another corner.

What good had it done to be so stressed out and nervous all the time? Damon Marcher might have been in prison, but all her worry about him using his outside influences to come after her again had been a waste of time. He was dead, and Amber was now the target of King and Lopez, both free and running the streets, as if they'd never left.

Sensing Ronni was in the restroom with her, Mia cursed the tears that flooded her eyes. Agent Punto had probably never cried in front of anyone, much less tossed her cookies during a meeting.

The sound of water filled the space. A wad of wet paper towels appeared a moment later above the top of the door. "Take your time," Ronni told her.

Mia reached for the towels, gratefully accepting them. She pressed the cool, damp paper against her hot cheeks and swelling eyes. They smelled, but the coolness was welcome.

Her throat was raw. She swallowed several times, waiting for her chest to constrict, for the next anxiety attack. While her breath hitched on silent sobs, the low-level fear she usually felt under her skin when one was imminent didn't rise. Her chest continued to expand and contract normally, if a bit tight. In fact, as the tears waned and she continued sucking in gulps of air, her mind cleared.

Once her legs finally felt stable, she opened the stall and stepped out. Ronni deftly took the old towels, replacing them with fresh ones. "You look better," she claimed.

"You're kind." Mia's reflection in the mirror over the sink told a different story. She wiped her face again, blowing out a long, slow breath. "I'm sure you're an outstanding agent, but you need your eyes checked."

Ronni grinned at her. "You walked in looking like a corpse. Now you've got color in your cheeks and hellfire in your eyes. You ready to go find your sister and put these bastards away for good?"

Mia found she could smile. Only a little, and her legs trembled as she did it, but she was tired of living in fear, tired of the anxiety attacks. "Tell me the truth, have you ever worked a kidnapping?"

Ronni gave a confident nod. "More than I care to admit. Hostage situations like this are one of my specialties."

Mia feared the answer to her next question but asked anyway. "What are her chances? Be honest. Do you really believe we'll get her back alive?"

The agent held her gaze, steady eyes open and honest. "Mia, there are too many variables in situations such as this when we don't know the motive or have confirmation of who the culprits are."

"I've confirmed it's the Quattro Gang."

Ronni gave her a patient smile. "They technically don't exist anymore, but granted, some of the players are still out there."

Mia huffed. "Give it to me straight." She understood that none of these people wanted her to lose hope, but she needed to know. "Your best guess. What are the odds we save her?"

A tense silence fell between them, but Ronni didn't break eye contact. "Fifty-fifty, and that's based on the fact we have the best agents in Southern California in that room. If she has any chance of surviving, it will be because of us. And you."

The fear and horror tried to rise again, but Mia slapped both away. *I'm coming, Amber.* She tossed the wet towels into the bin by the door, ran her fingers through her hair to tame her wild locks, then rinsed her mouth with a palmful of water.

Her reflection now showed a different woman, still upset but focused. Ronni was right—hellfire burned in her eyes. She was no longer riddled with anxiety. She was her old self once more—bold, brave, confident.

She opened the door and nodded at the other woman. "All right, let's go figure out how to rescue my sister."

TEN

By 0300 hours, they were all yawning and had gone over every possible scenario their tired brains could conceive of. Marcher had never given up the location he'd held Mia at, and they were no closer to figuring it out.

Malachi watched her from the corner of his eye, noting she'd returned from the bathroom with renewed vigor and determination, but that had long faded, exhaustion getting the best of her.

Dupé had flooded Bobby's inbox with reports ranging from traffic cams and possible newly recruited QG members, to intelligence reports concerning the many and varied businesses Damon Marcher had set up, run, and or taken over in the ten-plus years he'd been scheming and building his empire. Lots of shell corporations the Bureau still hadn't completely sorted out, and plenty of foreign companies they couldn't access.

The average citizen had known little to nothing about him, even with his legitimate companies. Still, he'd gathered secrets on every politician, CEO, and celebrity he could and used it to blackmail plenty of them. And as he quietly disposed of his enemies on the street and grew his international enterprises, he made sure he had numerous police officers, judges, and San Diego's movers and shakers under his thumb.

Marcher had no dirt on Amber Livingston, and she'd held out against his threats of personal harm, according to all reports. She'd made it clear when she took office that she would not cave to anyone's demands and would make it a priority to weed people like him, and his encroaching organization, out of the city.

It had nearly cost her Mia.

"The mayor received a lot of threats. One to harm her sister in a note with an undisclosed email address on May seventeenth may have been from Marcher." Bobby hit a couple keys on his laptop, sending a scan of the note to everybody's cells. "It's possible he had an undercover asset in the mayor's staff."

"My sister picked her advisors and staff personally. They all loved her." But Mia blanched as she read the note, her eyes going over and over the last sentence. "'If you refuse to cooperate, the cub dies.' Why do you think the writer is talking about me?"

"Marcher saw anyone in position, including himself, as a lion," Sam explained. "Top of the food chain in the wild. He referred to his own men as cubs. It fits."

"Why am I just seeing this now?" Her voice shook. Malachi wanted to reach for her. She glanced at Bobby, then around the circle. "No one ever showed this to me, or told me about it, after I was rescued."

Sam cleared her throat. "From my understanding, the mayor instructed the agents on the case not to share upsetting details."

Mia paled again. "But I deserved to know."

Malachi could no longer resist and touched her arm. "You

did. Maybe Amber intended to tell you eventually, but never found the right moment."

Ronni nodded in agreement. "Marcher was an asshole and a powerful one. We've got King, Lopez, and Damon's son, Newt, wanting to step into his shoes now. It takes a lot to keep an empire like his running. That group should have better things to do than kidnap the mayor for what appears to be revenge."

Malachi scrubbed a hand over his face. "What other agenda would they have?"

Mann kicked back in his seat, yawning toward the ceiling. "It smells like a set up to me."

"Setting up who?" Harris asked. It sounded like a challenge, but then, didn't most things when they came from the Taskforce leader?

Mann rubbed the back of his neck and shrugged. "If I were Jam King and I thought I could outsmart the Feds, take out Newt Marcher, and establish myself as the next boss in town, what better way than to throw the Feds into chaos than searching for the mayor? Meantime, I serve her up to Newt for revenge on his father, as well as showing my rivals I'm willing to take on anyone to lock in my place as the new leader of the Quattro gang."

Mia glanced at Malachi. "But he's going back to prison, right? Even if he gets what the FBI needs to arrest Newt, he's just the carrot on the end of the stick."

"Only if we catch him," Harris grumbled.

"What do you mean?" she asked.

Mann closed his eyes and crossed his arms over his chest. "He's got a tracker, but those can be manipulated. If he dodges the Feds, we'll never catch him. Damon excelled at keeping multiple identities well guarded. He had layers and layers of security, for both his legitimate and illegitimate businesses. All

King has to do is tap into that, establish himself on the street, and most of the old members who are still walking free will be back in action before any of us can spit."

Harris tapped a thumb against the table, his gaze on his coffee cup. "He'll probably spend most of his time out of the country, somewhere with soft extradition laws, and he'll run the companies remotely."

Mia put her face in her hands. Malachi could feel her disheartenment. Ladybug whined and Malachi patted Mia's leg. "How about we take a break and reconvene in a while? We could all use some fresh air."

Harris glanced over, sizing up Mia. "Cahill's right. Meet back here at 0800 hours. We'll come back to the drawing board. Bobby? Continue checking through traffic cam footage to see if we can find a trail for those SUVs. Thomas, walk Ronni through possible places Marcher had his disposal buildings located. I'll keep Dupé informed of our progress."

Mia didn't so much as budge. "I want to stay. There has to be something I can do."

Sam tossed down her pen. "There really isn't, and I wish there was. I'll look through aerial photos of the city to see if anything pops up for potential disposal places. I'm not ruling out the other possibilities we initially came up with—the florists and the butcher shops. Maybe even funeral homes—they certainly fit the bill. Joe can help me dig for any in the area that might have been owned by Marcher's shell corporations. We'll also look for places with walk-in size coolers and loading docks."

Ronni rose and started picking up coffee cups. "The best thing you can do, Mia, is get some rest. You need it. You'll be clear and more focused after a few hours of sleep."

"I don't need any," Mia muttered and then yawned. When

Ronni smiled at her, she shrugged. "Okay, maybe I do. I also need to feed Ladybug and Taz."

"Taz?" Malachi asked.

"Tasmania, my cat." She leaned back and stretched her arms over her head, then made a face. "I smell like I could use a shower, too."

Malachi thought she smelled of roses and honey. "I'm not sure your home is secure."

She stood and shook out her legs. "It's off the books and registered under my other identity, Amy Newsome. Not even Amber knew that. It's probably the safest place I could be right now."

He shoved himself upright, glad to stretch his legs as well. "Are you sure about that? It seems Amber knew a lot more than you realized."

A tiny crease formed between her brows, letting him know that irritated her. "That may be true, but I'm still pretty sure she didn't have a clue where I lived." She appeared sad. "We haven't even had dinner in the past year. Last night was the first time I've seen her in person since the trial."

His heart pinched for her. Not only had she been through a horrible experience, she'd been living like someone in witness protection, not even able to turn to her family afterward for normal moral support. They'd all kept their distance to protect her, but not being able to be around your loved ones, to not be able to share a hug or meal, felt like another form of torture to him.

They dispersed; luckily, the Taskforce office had maintained its covert status, so no reporters or other parties waited outside. Problem was, Malachi didn't have his truck.

The cool, early morning air was refreshing, although thunder boomed in the distance. As he and Mia realized they had no vehicle, Ronni emerged and tossed him a set of keys. "Blue Mazda down the street there." She pointed.

"I can text for a lift," Mia offered, digging out her phone, around Ladybug's body.

"No," Malachi and Ronni said at the same time. Malachi put his hand on hers and explained. "You're all over the news again. We can't use any kind of public transport or risk someone recognizing you."

She looked deflated. "Right, sorry. Old habit."

Malachi jingled the keys at Ronni. "Thanks. We'll work out a way to get your car to you as soon as possible."

She told him it was no problem, disappearing back inside. The two of them walked to the vehicle, both quiet. Ladybug snored in Mia's arms. Both the lady and the dog had been through hell in the past few hours. "I would offer to hide you at my place," Malachi said, "but I'm guessing my sudden celebrity status will have plenty of folks camped out there, hoping to catch me coming and going."

"Mine is best," she assured him. "It's a total dive, I have to warn you, but it's also a secret. We'll be protected there."

When they arrived a few minutes later, he said, "You weren't kidding."

The façade of the three story building was a faded gray, the ground floor windows barred. There was no parking, except on the street, and that was clogged with rusty and worn out vehicles from end to end. He feared leaving the shiny, nearly new Mazda out in the open, but he had no choice. He parked a block over, near a nicer looking neighborhood, then he walked Mia, with her hood up, to her apartment.

The entry and staircase resembled a frat house after a kegger, but her tiny one bedroom on the top floor was nice. It didn't stink like body odor and stale beer as the rest of the building did. In fact, it smelled of her.

Ladybug, awake now, was thrilled to be home. She ran in lopsided circles around the familiar digs. An elderly cat eyed Malachi suspiciously from her perch near a window, but then ignored him completely as Mia put a scoop of wet food in a bowl. Ladybug inhaled her kibble and flopped down on a dog bed immediately afterward, falling fast asleep once more.

"Can I get you a drink?" Mia asked. "Maybe something to eat? I don't keep much on hand, but..."

He could see her consternation. "Don't worry about me." He began checking the doors and windows to be sure they were locked up tight. Mia followed. "I'll just hang out on the couch while you clean up," he told her.

She looked a bit shy and embarrassed as they made their way through her room. He stayed professional, even when he saw her underwear scattered about. There were a few pictures on a desk, a stack of books next to her bed. That perfume, though, the roses and honey, was stronger here, permeating everything. He made busy work of inspecting the fire escape, then locking that window, along with pulling the shade and curtains.

Turning back and seeing her clothes, he mentally grinned as she grabbed a pair of red underwear from a nearby chair and hid them behind her back. Even after the day she'd had, she was still the sexiest thing he'd seen in a long time, but he didn't want her to feel he was taking advantage of her.

Her current state was vulnerable, and he would never do that to her. The last thing he wanted was to embarrass her, or make her feel uncomfortable in her own home.

So far, he'd been pretty good about shutting off his attraction to her, but now that he was standing here? Hell, if he could make it through the next few minutes, listening to her shower without imagining her naked under the water and dripping wet when she emerged, he deserved a gold star.

Feeling a hard-on already starting, he flopped into a chair in the living room with his back to her and grabbed the TV remote. "Yep," he called. "I'll be right here, watching the news."

He sensed her move close, and before he knew it, she leaned over and kissed the top of his head. "Thank you for helping me. For saving me and Ladybug."

Heat shot straight to his groin, but when he turned to say it was nothing, she'd already vanished into the bathroom.

Blowing out a slow, controlled breath, he texted Caleb. *Tell me something good.*

His brother didn't text back, but called. "Bro," Caleb's voice was slow like he'd been asleep. He probably had been. "Status?"

Malachi filled him in. "We're at her place, everything seems normal. Got anything as far as leads on your end?"

"Working on King and Lopez—trying to get locations. The Bureau claims King is staying with his girlfriend on the east side and never left tonight, but he's too smart to go after Amber himself. No one has a trace on Lopez. If those two are tied up in this, I bet he was part of the squad. Bobby is expanding his search to look for vehicles they may have traded off for, knowing those black SUVs used in the attack would be hot."

"I was thinking about something Thomas said regarding King wanting to step into Marcher's shoes. Can you get a list of those who visited King or Damon in prison?"

"According to Joe, Sam's already got one. It's pretty sad, really. Their only visitors were their lawyers and Newt saw his dad once. Nobody cared about either of them, I guess."

Malachi thought there was probably a different reason, but he couldn't grasp exactly what it was at the moment. His brain was too tired. "King's girlfriend never went to see him?"

"Nope. Bet she got a shock when he showed up on her doorstep yesterday."

The water came on in the other room. Malachi thumbed through channels. The early morning shows were starting to kick into gear. He rubbed his eyes with the back of his hand. "I bet she did, unless she knew something was up, or King told her to stay away because the Bureau was watching."

"What are you thinking?"

Mostly that he needed sleep. "What if King ordered the hit on Marcher?"

Caleb was quiet while he considered it. "Sticking with the theory he wanted to pave the way to take over? Tough to do when you're behind bars."

Malachi's brain was circling closer to the idea he was trying to grasp. "But not impossible."

A few seconds of quiet went by. He tried to keep his eyes open and focused on the news as his brother digested it. "I can see it working. Especially if he had the right connections and support inside."

Malachi and Caleb could usually read each other's minds pretty· easily. "You mean, like another gang?" Malachi questioned.

"Good way to get your feet in the door if you're small or new to this area. You leech onto a bigger gang, as they often do in prison, prove yourself to the leader—in this case, the lieutenant who wants his boss taken out—then the next thing you know, you have street cred and power that could have taken years to accomplish on your own."

Exactly.

"Isn't that what Lopez did?" Caleb continued. "He ran with the Diamond Dogs before he changed allegiances and killed their leader for Marcher."

"Yep, and King could have been passing messages through his attorney to Lopez to the stragglers left from the Quattro Gang. They needed fresh blood, after Marcher's bust, so Lopez recruited a young, hungry group to join them with the promise of instant status if they took out Marcher."

"King couldn't have known the Feds would offer the deal, though."

Malachi gave up the fight, closing his eyes and leaned back, sagging in the chair. "I haven't worked through all of that, yet, but I'd like to know the timeline and who suggested the deal. Was it the Bureau or King's lawyer? I also want a list of new and upcoming gangs in the area, both those in prison and on the street. Remember the skip we had that ran a pet shop? He was tied up with the Komosu, wasn't he?"

"The Koreans. Yeah, at night he worked the gambling dens for them. They moved fake antiquities and guns, laundering the money through the store."

It didn't seem to jive with the guy he'd confronted, or Lopez, but the others had been Korean, he was sure of it. He had that niggling buzz under his chest bone that suggested the two were related. "Granted, it's a long shot, but they were greedy and ruthless, two attributes King and Lopez admire."

The clicking of keys came through the connection, as Caleb must have sat down at his computer. "Hmm. The guy who took out Marcher is named Han Beak. Doesn't ring a bell, but I'll do more digging, see what he's in for, and if he has connections to any gangs. Who doesn't these days? Could be our missing link."

It didn't help them find Amber, but they were holding jack squat in that area. There had to be a thread in this ball of twine that could be pulled to unwind it. "Sounds good. Keep me posted."

"Get some sleep."

"Roger that." He disconnected, tossed the phone on the coffee table, and side-eyed the cat who had jumped onto the rear of the couch. She proceeded to lick a paw and clean her face, keeping a golden gaze locked on him.

The shower made a soft drone in the background. No matter how hard he tried to keep his lids open to concentrate on the news and kidnapping, his mind continually wandered to Mia. His imagination refused to be tamed, and he let the movie reel play.

He was a cad, but he couldn't help it. He saw her skin pebble under the water, saw her dark lashes damp with drops, those intense green eyes beckoning him. They were real, those eyes, and damn if they didn't turn him on.

He wanted to hold her, cradle her, reassure her. Under it all, he wanted to remove the fear and disillusionment from them and help her forget, even if only for a few minutes, that anything was wrong. If only he could worship her body and bring her some relief.

As the water lulled him, and the television murmured on, Malachi's mind shifted into dreams of desire-filled green eyes and all the ways he'd like to worship Mia Livingston's body.

ELEVEN

When Mia emerged from the steamy bathroom, she was met with Malachi's snores. There was nothing timid about them either. They permeated her tiny apartment, practically rattling the windows, and made her chuckle.

Tucking her robe tighter around her, she tiptoed past the chair, a goofy smile on her lips. The big guy filled her place with his larger than life presence, not to mention those healthy snores, but he made her feel safe, secure.

Taz meowed softly as Mia sank down on the couch, tucking her legs up under her. She checked her phone, saw no messages, and slipped it back into her pocket. The TV was silenced. She ignored it while stroking the cat and thinking about the kiss she'd pressed on the top of Malachi's head.

It had been totally spontaneous, and she hoped not inappropriate. She didn't even know him—not really—but where would she be right now without him?

During her shower, she kept seeing him step in front of her and Ladybug during the attack. His light touches throughout the meeting had kept her grounded. Her heart warmed at the memory of his smile. He was the first man in a long, long time who had made her feel so...happy.

As she watched him sleep, she knew in her heart he was a good guy. He'd done more for her in the past few hours than most folks had in her entire lifetime. His whole team had welcomed her, and even though he hadn't told her the details of the deal the FBI had made with King upfront, she understood why—he'd been protecting her the best way he could. Amber had, too.

So much for worrying about breaking the news to him regarding who she was. He'd been slapped in the face with it before she'd even told him her name.

Worst first date ever.

Not a date, she reminded herself. She hadn't had one of those in nearly two years, and she didn't regret it one bit. She'd been too busy helping Amber make it to the mayor's office, then recovering from the kidnapping.

Now, because of his kindness, not to mention those muscles, certain *things* were stirred up. She wanted to feel like the twenty-seven-year-old that she was, not the shelled out person she'd become.

The throw pillow called to her. She had nothing left. Her body was shutting down. She nestled into the soft couch, tugging an afghan over her legs.

Her eyelids were heavy weights. Sleep could no longer be cheated. As the screen flickered over Malachi's strong features, she found herself smiling again. Her last view, as she finally gave up, was of him.

***

MIA WOKE to a buzzing vibration and the looping melody she reserved for Sue.

Neck stiff, she stifled a yawn, pushed upright and hurriedly shut off the ring tone. Malachi slept through it, his body contorted sideways in the chair now, head thrown back and mouth open. It was a funny thing to see him in such a carefree state. She didn't want to wake him.

The message from Sue was short and sweet. *I'm here. You okay?*

Damn it. Mia had told Sue she'd need a lift at eight every morning this week. Sue only knew her as Amy and had no idea who she was, or that what had happened to the mayor would alter Mia's need for a drive. Mia cringed with guilt that she'd forgotten to cancel.

Ladybug managed to stand, still in her dog bed, and shook herself as Mia replied. *So sorry! I forgot to cancel. I'll send payment through anyway! A.*

What came back was a frown-y face response. *No worries, but I do have your favorite muffins and a treat for Ladybug if you want them.*

Mia bit her bottom lip. Any other day, she would have shot down the stairs in record time to retrieve them. The double chocolate variety from Be Mine Bakery was something both she and Sue indulged in once a month.

Trying to formulate a significant excuse was more challenging than expected. She typed, deleted, started again. Then she gave up, went to her payment app, and added a generous tip.

Except, when she hit send, the app crashed. She swore, then hurriedly tried again. No deal. The program was having issues.

Great, now she couldn't even compensate the woman.

Ladybug shuffle-walked around, sniffing at Malachi's hand, flopped over the arm of the chair and dragging on the floor. Mia glanced at the sleeping man and chewed her lip again. She had to take Ladybug out anyway. *Be right there*, she told Sue.

From her purse, she took out cash and her stun gun. Then she tightened her robe and picked up Ladybug.

The dog had to be carried but was anxious to get to the ground once they were outside the entrance. Mia shaded her eyes and glanced down the road. The sun was rising, though the neighborhood wasn't fully awake yet. A guy rode by on a bike, a woman ran along the opposite sidewalk with her Labrador, jogging in place when it stopped to mark a tree.

Ladybug barked a greeting. The woman waved and she and her canine companion continued on.

Everything looked normal. Mia breathed a sigh of relief.

Sue was parked in her usual spot, halfway down the block. Mia carried Ladybug with one hand, keeping her tucked close to her side, her other resting on the weapon inside her pocket. Nobody paid any attention as she closed the distance and crossed the street. Sue was texting when Mia knocked on the window. When she glanced up, she smiled and lowered it, tossing her phone in the seat. "Here you go," she said, handing Mia a bakery bag. "I'm sorry you don't need a ride. Everything okay?"

"Yep, just didn't need to go today."

"Oh my, what happened to you, Ladybug?" Sue scratched the dog's ears, and Ladybug preened.

Mia froze for a second. She hadn't thought about Ladybug and her injury giving them away, but it was a possibility if Sue had seen the video of the attack.

The dog wiggled and leaned in for more pets, showering Sue with air kisses.

"She went after a squirrel," Mia lied, juggling the bag and squirming dog. "Didn't win this round unfortunately. The vet said she'd be fine in short order."

"Did she break her leg?"

"Just a mild bruise."

Behind her sunglasses, Sue seemed to study them. She stroked the dog's ears. "Ladybug, you need to pick your battles. Did your job get canceled for the professor?"

Mia rolled her eyes and made something up. "Not quite, but his grant is on hold, so for now, he doesn't need me. You know how it goes."

Sue made a disgusted sound in the back of her throat. "Did you see the news about the mayor? What a terrible world we live in, isn't it? I sure hope she'll be okay."

Mia's heart tripped over itself. "They'll find her," she said with as much confidence as she could muster. She wasn't sure if it was for herself or Sue. "The app crashed, so here's cash."

"Thanks." She accepted it and tucked it into a bag she kept near her leg. "You look like you took on a few squirrels yourself. You good?"

Mia stepped away, stomach falling. She hated lying again, but what else could she do? "I was up late, searching for another research job. Gotta run. See ya!"

Stupid! What was I thinking?

Before she made it back across the street to the apartment, her stomach fell even farther.

Malachi stood in the entrance to her building, scowling like an angry bear.

TWELVE

Malachi's oh-shit meter went Code Red when he woke up and couldn't find Mia. Like in the Marines, it had sent warning messages all up and down his central nervous system.

The missing dog, however, had given him pause. Through his blurry daze and stiff neck, he had realized Mia had most likely taken Ladybug out for her morning constitutional.

Still, even that was dangerous at the moment, and he wished she'd waited for him.

It was his fault for falling asleep on her, and not even waking when she'd left the apartment this morning. He hadn't slept like that in... Well, it had been a damn long time.

Maybe even before he'd joined the military. That was saying something, but he didn't have time to analyze it now.

As Mia hustled toward him, Ladybug cradled in her arms, he breathed a relieved sigh. She had to pause and wait for a passing vehicle, and as she did so, he noticed her tight features. She wouldn't meet his eyes. Something had spooked her.

Down the block, an older Subaru sat parked, the driver

watching Mia in the rearview. Malachi's warning system started up all over again.

She jogged to him, giving him a shaky smile. "Good morning."

He reined in the lecture he wanted to give her and tried to smile back. A white bag bounced in her grip. Ladybug's tail wagged hard. Gently taking her by the elbow, he cast surreptitious glances around. The sidewalk and street were fairly empty but wouldn't be for long. The Subaru idled at the curb. He mentally noted the license plate number.

Instead of directing Mia through the main entrance, he led her to the side. The path here was overgrown with weeds and empty beer cans. "Who's the woman you were talking to?"

Mia seemed confused, more about their trajectory than his question. "She's a driver for WeGo. I booked her to take me to the university all week and forgot to cancel." She hefted the bag. "We have muffins for breakfast, thanks to her."

Malachi took it and motioned for Mia to stay put. A glance around the corner assured him the driver had gone. "She could have recognized you from the video."

Mia gave him a regretful nod. "I know. I didn't think about that. I felt bad that I'd forgotten to cancel, and then the app wouldn't work to pay her. Plus, these muffins are to die for." She set the wiggling terrier down. The dog limp-walked to a bush and sniffed. "Sue's a good person, and no one's after me. They took Amber. Besides, I'm done hiding."

She removed a stun gun and flashed it at him. He held his tongue. That pee-wee might take out a single mugger, but not a group of trained men like those they were dealing with. She was right, though—it seemed whoever attacked them wasn't after her. "Even if no one from the Quattro Gang or those douchbags from last night are looking for you, the press may be. You still need to lay low and keep off the grid."

Her defiant chin lifted as she returned the weapon to her pocket. The sash of her robe fell loose to reveal creamy skin peeking from a crop top and a pair of flowery shorts. "Granted, you may be right, but even if Sue figured out who I am, she's not going to go blabbing it around. We're friends. Sort of."

Ladybug made her way over to Malachi. He scooped her up. He had multiple texts from Harris, Sam, and Caleb, but he hadn't taken time to read them in his haste to search for Mia. He hoped at least one was good news. "These better be worth exposing yourself for."

A genuine grin lit her face. "You do like chocolate, right?"

Of course they wouldn't be anything healthy. Unless the Taskforce wrapped up this hostage situation in a few days, his goal of being ready for the triathlon was slim. If they got Amber back unharmed, he'd trade it with no regrets. "I'm not big on sweets, honestly." He directed her to the rear entrance. "But chocolate has been known to pass my lips."

She hiked up her robe to step over some ground cover that had long ago turned wild and waved around their knees in the breeze. "Well, you're in for a treat."

The amount of stunning cleavage on display certainly was a treat. Along with those legs, he was right back to where he'd been a few hours ago, mental fantasies running crazy. He forced his eyes away, but that image was burned in his mind, right along with her smile.

"Malachi?"

He'd frozen with his hand on the knob. Glancing up, he kept his gaze on her face. "Yes?"

"You okay?"

I haven't been awestruck by breasts since high school. "Sure." He nodded profusely, pinning his eyes on the far wall as he held the door open for her. "Let's get you upstairs."

Back in her apartment, he replied to the messages while

Mia dug out two plates and started coffee. None of them provided the information he'd been hoping for.

He tried not to watch as Mia fed the animals and gave Ladybug her medication, the silk robe tantalizing him, and that damned sash refusing to stay tied as she bent to take care of them. Once they were set, she stretched to grab two mugs, and it came loose again. Even when she re-tied it, cutting off the view, the material flowed over her curves, like warm syrup, outlining her butt, those generous breasts.

Cooper's text directed him not to bother bringing Mia to the office at eight. No real progress had been made on tracking her sister. Along with a city-wide manhunt by law enforcement, Thomas had been calling on his snitches to find info on the underground grapevine. No one was talking—either because they didn't know any details, or were too scared to cough them up.

Sam had narrowed a search parameter to five possibilities for Marcher's disposal place. Dupé was putting in orders for SWAT teams to check them out later that day.

Caleb's message was two words: *call me*.

"Ready?" Mia stood at the table with two mugs of the steaming brew in hand.

"Sorry I fell asleep on you." He covertly scanned her hair, her face, her hands as he casually walked to one of the chairs. She had bedhead and her skin was bare of makeup. Dark circles were under her eyes and the strain showed in the tiny crease between her brows. She had delicate fingers, like a pianist. He took a seat, then raised an eyebrow. "Is this yours?"

It took her half a second to get the joke, and she stuck out her tongue. Ladybug barked, as if laughing. "No, smartass." She set the mug in front of his plate, then took the chair opposite. "You got it right this time."

He gave her a big grin and dug in. As they ate, he brought

her up to date on what Coop and Sam had reported. Her good mood vanished as she toyed with her breakfast. "I want to go with the SWAT team."

"Can't. Dupé will never allow it."

Her eyes pleaded with him across the table. "What if they find her? I have to be there for her."

There was no way the Feds would permit a civilian to attend a raid. Plus, Malachi had no idea which was the most likely of the five locations the teams were being dispatched to. "I'm hoping my brother has a lead," he told her in an effort to distract her. "I also need him to bring me a set of fresh clothes."

Her face fell, but she tried to cover her disappointment by teasing him. "No judgment, but you are a bit ripe. I can wash your things, you know. There's a laundry facility downstairs, and you're welcome to use my shower."

The muffin was definitely worth the sugar and calories. He finished off a bite and appreciated the fact she would do that for him. "Let's see what Caleb has for information. Then we can fix my smelly situation."

She sipped her coffee, then picked at her food. "The two of you are a lot alike in appearance, but you seem...more mature. I mean, I really don't know either of you that well, but I can tell he looks up to you. They all do. You and Caleb are very different people."

Thank god for that. "Our parents raised us to be individuals, and we really are."

A ringing sounded from her robe, and Mia startled. Setting down the cup, she drew her phone from her pocket. "It's Professor G. Crud, I have to tell him I can't get his work done. He'll want to know why. What should I say?"

Malachi shook his head. "Let it go to voicemail for now. We'll figure out what to tell him shortly and you can call back."

She sank into the chair, pushing the cell away. "This could ruin my reputation as a research admin."

He touched her arm, "This is putting a kink in a lot of things, but we'll figure it out after we get Amber."

She groaned, a raw sound from deep inside. "What is wrong with me? Here I am worrying about my job when Amber could be..." Her voice cracked.

"Your sister is going to be okay." He hit his speed dial for Caleb. "And I have faith that you will be, too."

His twin answered on the first ring, and Malachi put him on speaker. "I found something interesting. It's not much, but it could lead us to the big fish in this situation."

"What?" he and Mia asked at the same time, then shared a grin.

"The guy who stabbed Marcher, Han Beak?"

Mia hadn't heard that conversation. She held up her hands at him in question. He raised a finger to let her know he'd catch her up later. "What about him?"

Caleb cleared his throat. "His real identity is Hun Baek. Baek is a Korean surname and he simply switched the letters up. Guess who he used to work for?"

The lightbulb went on in Malachi's brain. "Tell me it's Komosu."

"Bingo." He heard Caleb shifting around, papers shuffling. "Still working on that timeline, bro, but we're onto something. Oh, and that other thing?"

"Yeah?"

"King's girlfriend used to be Beak's."

"What? That doesn't make sense."

"She visited him before he killed Marcher."

The gang world was small, when you got right down to it, and Malachi felt that tiny buzz under his shoulder blades.

"What do you want to bet she's not King's?" Malachi theorized. "I bet he's holding her as collateral."

Mia looked lost and gestured at him impatiently. "I don't understand any of this."

He hadn't found that thread he'd been searching for exactly, but he knew they were getting close, all the moving parts were going to come together. He needed to talk to Coop, get that timeline nailed down.

First he needed a shower and more caffeine. "Does Joe still have all that stuff at his house?"

"You mean the wigs and shit?"

"Yeah."

"Far as I know, why? You're not thinking about going undercover are you?"

"Not my speed." Malachi eyed Mia. "But we do need a disguise."

THIRTEEN

The morning fog along the coast enveloped Malachi's truck. Ronni had brought it by to exchange for her car, and now Mia, Malachi, and Ladybug were on their way north to Joe and Sam's house in Carlsbad.

Mia felt disheartened that they hadn't found Amber, and a phone call with her parents, who were now in town, had made her feel worse.

There was no comforting her mother, who'd cried through the whole thing, while Mia's dad had raged in the background about why this was happening to their family.

He hated politics, couldn't believe his eldest daughter had chosen that path. He and Amber were like night and day, always butting heads, but Mia knew their father loved them to the bottom of his soul.

Malachi had told her he was convinced he was onto something. He laid out his ideas as they drove. "When a gang's leadership is decimated like Quattro's, it leaves a void." He shifted into another lane, passing a slow moving vehicle. "Criminals don't like those. In general, they are opportunists, and although none of them have quite the right combination of resources and leadership to fully take over Marcher's place, they all want one thing."

Ahead, dark clouds hung over the interstate. "Power," Mia guessed.

He nodded. "It's likely Jam King has been waiting for the right moment to take out Damon and claim his empire. But he got tripped up when Marcher went after you, and that bubble burst. Marcher wanted control of the highest office in the city— the mayor's—but he didn't have any dirt to make your sister bend to his will. She wouldn't be blackmailed, but he'd grown so egotistical, he thought he could kidnap you and force her to cave in to his demands."

She thought about the threatening note that Amber had kept hidden from her. It still galled her. *I'm no cub.* And whoever had taken Amber was going to pay for this.

On the other hand, the mayor— regardless of who was in office—received threatening notes all the time. Had Amber even known it was from Damon? Had the FBI proven it came from him? Every politician had plenty of enemies, there were plenty of wackos out there, too. "She wouldn't cave to anyone's demands, and he couldn't kidnap me and keep it a secret."

"It seems personal to me, and that keeps bugging me, but it might not have been. Kidnapping you was his downfall. King may have even encouraged it, seeing a way to get Marcher out of the picture and create the void he needed."

She tried to think like the man next to her. "It backfired and King also ended up behind bars. He must not be all that smart."

"Don't underestimate him. He certainly didn't give up, biding his time to start working the angles. Even from prison, he had resources to lean on, the Quattro members who escaped arrest. All he needed was a way to unite them again. Once he laid that groundwork, he hired or blackmailed this Beak fellow to kill Damon. Risky by some counts, since he was incarcerated himself, but those previously loyal to Marcher were sure to look to King for guidance. He was the face of the gang, not Marcher."

"Marcher hid behind his companies."

"Exactly."

The fog and clouds made her feel chilled. Or maybe it was the conversation. She stroked Ladybug's chest. "I know it happens, but it seems challenging to run a criminal organization from jail."

Malachi's hand on the steering wheel gripped it loosely. "It actually has a few advantages."

She shot him an incredulous look, rubbing her arms with her hands.

He adjusted the air vents, dialing up the temperature a few degrees. "We don't have to get into that right now, but Marcher had gang members in with him, and prisoners are industrious. I doubt it was hard for him to mete out orders and keep things running. Men like Marcher attract people looking for power. Much like your sister. The Bureau confiscated the assets they could find, but according to the reports, not everything. His businesses— both legitimate and not— exist all over the world, under many other names and shell companies. He still had plenty of money, as well as power, and his followers knew it. Now King has taken up the mantle, if he can get free and disappear. The only thing in his way is Newt."

"You mentioned that King was holding Beak's girlfriend as collateral. Why would he do that?"

"To ensure Han doesn't turn on him. King takes care of her, brings the Komosu into the Quattro family, and adds foot soldiers to his ranks. Then he gets the Feds to release him for this supposed covert op, and recruits his old buddy Lopez to reel in Newt. Marcher's son is most likely sitting on the many assets his father kept hidden—and he may not even realize it."

The cab grew shadowed, visibility worse as a light rain fell. Mia massaged her temples. "It's too convoluted for me. Too…"

"Criminal?"

She nodded, relieved he understood.

Malachi turned on the wipers and headlights. "King wants what Damon had. Damon ends up in prison, King hires the Komosu to kill him, thereby leaving the leadership of the gang, and a whole lot of assets, free for the taking—if he can get Newt out of the way. King gets what he wants, re-emerging down the road with a fresh identity and a well-established organization to run. Men have killed for a lot less."

She liked how he laid it out so methodically. She knew little about this world, and his breakdown kept her from feeling totally ignorant.

His face was as handsome in profile as it was straight on. She snuck peeks at him, admiring his strong jaw and broad shoulders. "And kidnapping Amber? You think it's this Komosu crew, proving their loyalty? Like some kind of initiation? You said they were Korean—the person who dragged her out of the limo and threatened me, was not. He was QC, I'm sure of it."

The rain began to fall in earnest and Malachi increased the speed of the wipers. "It could have been a joint venture—that guy might have been along to make sure things went as planned. I have a feeling it was more than an initiation, but I'm not sure what else just yet."

She asked the question that continued to niggle at her. "Why not take me, too?"

He glanced over and must have seen her guilt. His big hand reaching out to grasp hers. "I know this is tough, Mia. You weren't the target this time because the goal is different. You can't blame yourself."

"For some weird reason, I do."

Maybe it was a twisted version of survivor's guilt. At the peer meetings, attendees sometimes talked about that. One of the regulars brought up how he had survived a shooting while his three best friends hadn't. He felt he didn't deserve to live, and he had no explanation for why he hadn't even been grazed by a bullet when the gunman opened fire.

Malachi's caress was gentle, light. It always was. She hadn't been touched in a long time except for the hug Amber had crushed her with last night at finally seeing her face-to-face. It felt exhilarating, welcome even, but she also felt shy.

There were moments his hand on her wasn't enough. She wanted to be embraced, held, comforted. All the while the guilt kept pushing her needs aside.

Oh, who was she kidding? She wanted more than just to be held. If she was going to start living again— really living, she needed love, intimacy, passion. Even if Malachi hadn't possessed a big sexy brain to go along with his muscles, she would have wanted to jump him. The fact he did?

Look out, big guy.

But now wasn't the time. When this was over and Amber was home safe and sound—Mia had to cling to that thought— Malachi and her libido were going to square off.

Turning her hand to entwine her fingers with his, she clutched it and let his warmth sink into her skin. The faintest lift of his lips was there and gone when she did it. He didn't say anything or release his hold, as the rain continued and the wipers kept clearing the windshield, she didn't either.

"WOW." She couldn't think of anything more apt to say. Not only was Sam and Joe's house incredibly nice, the walk-in-closet was like a movie prop fitting room. "Do I want to know why they have all this stuff?"

"Sam used to do undercover work." Malachi leaned on the door behind him. Jack-Jack was the only one home, he happily greeted them. He was currently giving Ladybug a downstairs tour.

Mia fingered the assortment of clothes on their hangers, from swanky ball gowns to blue jeans and leather jackets. It was like playing dress-up with a millionaire's wardrobe, rather than your grandmother's abandoned trunk in the attic. "WITSEC could take lessons from Sam." During and after Marcher's trial, they'd set her up with a minimum of image altering choices. The hair dye, colored contacts, told her to wear layers of bulky clothes to hide her thin frame.

In the full length mirror at the end of the room, she noticed her roots were showing. With her light brown hair that already had a reddish undertone, going auburn had been easy. Keeping up with it, however, not so much. She'd been wearing contacts for years, changing out her eye color had been simple. She'd stopped wearing make-up, stopped caring about her appearance, instead trying to disappear.

In the center there was a table with a marble countertop. It seemed to be a sort of dresser, with multiple shelves that rolled out. She glanced at Malachi across it then back to the clothes. Could he look any sexier, leaning casually against the doorjamb? Neither of them had mentioned the hand holding; she considered bringing it up to clarify that she liked him, but she wasn't in to hook-ups and a relationship was... well, rushing it.

She definitely wanted one when things calmed down, if it ever did. But her life was a hot mess at the moment. The idea of dating appealed, yet she couldn't shake off the weight on her shoulders. She was literally filled with scars inside and out, and wasn't that a great way to start off with a new guy? Of course,

Malachi knew about some of them, but not all of them, by a long shot.

The thing was, she sensed she didn't need to say that. She wasn't the only one with scars. He'd been at that meeting, and while some might say it was serendipity, she hoped it was more than that.

She'd always been good at speaking, her gift for communication making her a great speech writer for Amber. Now, she wasn't sure how to articulate any of this without sounding like a victim or martyr. Neither role sat comfortably, nor did she want to embrace either. She just wasn't sure what her new position was. It all felt undecided, as though she were in limbo.

He continued to remain quiet, watching her examine the handbags, the shoes. She paused at a selection of wigs. "What do you think." She pointed at the blonde style with bangs, then a brunette pageboy. "Which would suit me better?"

His gaze didn't leave her face, and she felt his awareness of her down to her toes. "You're beautiful the way you are."

Parts of her lower body lit up like someone had struck a match. Parts that had been dead a long time. Outside, the rain continued in soft sheets, she felt as though they were in another world. A different time and place.

Or maybe that was just her wishful thinking. "But this isn't my natural color."

"I'm not talking about that. You could rock pink hair with rainbow stripes and I'd still find you beautiful."

Her breath lodged inside her chest. Heat raced to her cheeks. "You're not bad yourself."

A dark brow arched and the corner of his mouth twitched. "Is that so?"

Before her brain could caution her, as it did constantly these days, she closed the distance between them. *What am I doing?* Shoving the analyzing away, she threw herself at him.

It was like jumping into a warm pool. He came out of his casual stance and was ready for her, his arms opening. He half lifted her off the floor, his mouth meeting her upturned one and their lips colliding.

Drowning. That's what this was. She circled his neck with her arms and shoved her hands through his hair. He moaned and kissed her, teasing her with the tip of his tongue, his strong muscles holding her tightly but tenderly.

She itched to touch him everywhere, to squeeze those muscles, to look inside his heart. She settled on running her fingers down his back and onto his shoulders as he probed the landscape of her mouth. Not drowning—he was her lifesaver on a sea of unknown.

"So damn beautiful," he muttered against her lips.

Her legs instinctively wrapped around his hips and he cupped her bottom. She continued to revel in the feel of him, letting the waves of emotion roll over her. Hard, strong, amazing, she reveled in the way he positioned her on the center island.

He broke the kiss, and they stared at each other, both breathing hard for a long moment. Then she was reaching for his shirt to tug it off.

Downstairs the dogs barked; they heard a beeping noise follow.

"Damn it," Malachi swore.

She released the grip on the hem of his shirt, suddenly on alert. "Is someone here?"

He backed away, lifting her and placing her carefully on her feet. "Joe has the worst timing."

Except it wasn't Joe. It was Sam.

They found her removing a raincoat in the hall. "Hey," she said. "Caleb told me you guys were here." She hung it in the mudroom then marched to the kitchen. Jack-Jack was jumping all over the place greeting her like she'd been away for years. She petted him as she looked them over. "You two okay? You look like you just ran an all-out sprint."

Mia fidgeted, feeling that heat in her cheeks again.

Malachi looked out the window, the corner of his mouth twitching again. "Any news? Do you have any leads for us?"

Sam's keen gaze floated between them. "Actually yes, which is why I'm here." She slapped a leather messenger bag on the breakfast bar, digging into it, pulling out a manila folder. Opening it, she laid out a line of photos on the marble. Some appeared to be satellite pictures of buildings, others of interior rooms.

She tapped one that showed an overhead shot of a property with multiple buildings. "This was a private lab back in the eighties. The Iranians were using ricin as a weapon, and this lab was contracted by our government to create the same type, and experiment with potential antidotes. Lots of cold storage units in here, as well as a furnace where they burnt anything that accidentally was exposed to the toxin, and cremated the lab animals they experimented on."

Mia flinched, "That's horrible."

Malachi came to peer over her shoulder. Mia naturally moved closer to him. He placed his arms around her, pointing at a blurry lot. The images of several vehicles were parked between them. "What's going on there? What is that next to the lab?"

"A landfill." Sam took out a report with the EPA's logo at the top, "It was tested by the EPA when the lab had to be shut down, both properties had ricin contamination. The techs were all exposed and most died. A clean-up crew was sent in and sanitized. The landfill was simply closed and marked as hazardous.

Mia glanced between the two of them. "So, what are you

saying? That you think this is somewhere Marcher used? That Amber could be there?"

Sam shoved another picture toward her. "There's a loading dock like you described, spaces used for experiments, a cremation room, and multiple buildings. The danger from the ricin is gone, but the property was a write-off. It's been abandoned for years, or so the government believed. No one wanted it. Except, satellite imagery shows activity suggesting someone has been using it again."

The tiny flame of hope Mia kept tending to grew. "Could Amber be there?"

Sam tapped a third and fourth aerial shot. "At least a dozen times since two thousand eighteen, vehicles were photographed by the NSA coming and going from the property, as well as smoke occasionally issuing from the crematorium. Nothing was ever confirmed and no one was caught when it was reported. Law enforcement believed it was homeless people or druggies using it to squat. It could have been Marcher and he used the landfill as well."

She still hadn't answered Mia.

"Makes it convenient to dump bodies." Malachi stated.

"That it is. Or at least their cremated remains. Best of all?" Sam gave Mia a direct look. "It's only eight miles away from where SPDP caught Marcher with you in the trunk, Mia."

The suffocating memory flashed through her mind. It had been dumb luck that her captor loaded her in his vehicle that night. He had something big planned—Mia suspected her death—he never anticipated a rookie cop pulling him over for a burned out taillight. She'd been delirious from starvation and torture, but she'd had an instinct to make as much noise as possible. Marcher had assumed she was passed out, but she'd gotten her revenge in the end by bloodying her hands and feet, hammering them on the lid and screaming through the gag in her mouth to catch the officer's attention.

Marcher had shot the policeman when he'd asked to see inside. Then her kidnapper had taken off. The cop's partner, still in the cruiser, jumped out and fired on Marcher's car. She remembered the high speed chase that followed, her body banging around in that dark trunk, her nose filled with the smell of moldy carpet and metal. By that time, she'd long since run out of tears, but the complete irony of being so close to salvation, only for Marcher to win again, had brought a fresh deluge. Along with them, she had screamed and screamed and screamed.

Marcher hadn't escaped, though, and she'd been rescued.

Sam touched her hand as a kind of solidarity. "We found three sites within the parameters we are looking, Dupé wants them all investigated, but I believe this location is our best bet. SWAT is heading there tonight at sunset."

"I want to be there."

Sam frowned. "I'm sorry, Mia. You're a civilian. It's too dangerous and Dupé will never okay it."

"I'm going."

Sam and Malachi exchanged a glance. Sam began to argue but Malachi intervened first. "She deserves to be there, but I understand where you're coming from. Dupé is right. It's too dangerous." He shifted Mia back a foot, tugging her close to his hip. "Thanks for keeping us informed, Sam. I know you'll contact us as soon as you learn anything from any of the sites."

Mia fumed. "Malachi, I have to be there if they find Amber." She tried to push away from him but he was too strong and kept her pinned against him. "What if it was Caleb or Joe?" She pointed at Sam. "If you were in my place, would you sit here on your hands and do nothing?"

Sam gave her a patient look. Malachi rubbed her shoulder,

drawing her aside, putting his back to the agent as she began gathering the photos. He winked at Mia and put a finger to his lips. "We'll head back to Mia's as soon as we find her a disguise," he told Sam.

Mia frowned, trying to shove him away, but he winked again and suddenly she got it.

He was misleading the agent.

A slow smile spread across her face, and when he saw her get it, he nodded slightly. She returned it. "Okay," she said. Secrets, disguises. A plan. Maybe she could do this after all.

Giving in too easily would make Sam suspicious. She squeezed Malachi's hand and then shifted to see the FBI agent who was going for her coat. "Will you please ask Director Dupé for me?"

If Sam smelled a rat, she didn't show it. She pulled on her outerwear and petted Jack-Jack once more. "Yes, I'll try, but don't get your hopes up. Keep your phones on and I'll call you the minute we know anything for sure." She offered Mia a sad smile. "It's the best I can do."

Mia felt Malachi put a hand on her shoulder. "I under-stand," she said again. "Thank you."

FOURTEEN

Malachi watched Sam drive away.

From the corner of his eye, he saw Mia bouncing on her toes, her eagerness overtaking common sense. "We're going to the raid, right?"

Turning, he put on his eldest brother, I'm-in-charge face. "On one condition."

She nodded enthusiastically. "Anything." No hesitation there. "Whatever you want."

His dirty mind instantly leaped to something with her in far fewer clothes, but he quashed it. The make-out session upstairs had his libido chomping at the bit, and he had to remind himself this wasn't the time.

He strode past her to retrieve a bottled water from the fridge. It wasn't a cold shower, but it would have to do to calm his raging hard-on.

Speaking of shower, he'd never gotten one. He'd managed to wash in her bathroom sink, but nothing beyond that. Joe's clothes were probably too tight in the chest, but he'd borrow a pair of loose sport pants and the biggest t-shirt he could find. That would have to do.

Ladybug barked and she and Jack-Jack looked expectantly at him, as well.

"Malachi, I'm serious," Mia chided. "We have to be there."

He took a long swig, considering his plan. "We could both end up in a lot of trouble with the FBI if we crash the party."

Her eyes burned with determination. "I don't really care. I mean, I get it if you don't want to burn bridges, but she's my sister. I will do anything to get her back and be there when we do."

He understood. He didn't care about pissing off Dupé, yet he was in charge of Bondsmen Brothers. Caleb, Joe, Josie and the other apprehension agents counted on him to keep things running smoothly. He was their leader, their CEO, fulfilling a role he felt born to. It's why he'd risen through the ranks so easily during his military days—he liked being in charge, and he had the strategic mind and innate sense to bring out the best in others.

Mia placed a hand on his stomach. "What's the condition?"

Her eyes had darkened and now resembled emeralds. It was foolish to give into her, but hell if he could say no. "You follow my lead, do what I say, and don't go renegade on me."

"That's three," she countered with a grin.

He lifted his brows and stared her down. "I'm serious. We'll remain on the sidelines, hidden. We're only there to observe, not engage. We'll stay clear of the action, understood? If it so happens that Amber *is* there, I'll do my best to make sure you get to see and speak to her once it's safe. If you so much as breathe when I've told you not to, I'll pull the plug and remove you from the scene, physically, if necessary. Are we clear?"

Her palm, burning through his shirt, dipped to his belt and she gave it a tug. "You're kinda bossy, you know that?"

It would be so easy to let her distract him, too easy. He grabbed her by the wrist, gently but firmly, and drew her hand away. It was hell to do it, since he wanted her so bad. "Swear it, Mia."

The playfulness left her voice. "Fine. I promise to follow your lead and all the other stuff. Do you know where this place is? Sam didn't give us the address."

"The coordinates were on the photos. I'll be able to find it after I shower."

She bit her bottom lip, as if considering what that entailed. "I'll feed Ladybug her meal and medicine, and find a disguise." The grin returned. "Is it okay to give Jack-Jack something? I hate to leave him out."

It was after lunch and Malachi needed a snack himself. The only thing that would truly satisfy him right now, though, wasn't food. "Kibble is in the pantry."

As she went to take care of the dogs, he grabbed his drink and snagged the first set of reasonable clothes he could find in Joe's closet. Inside the master bath, he turned on the dual heads and stripped.

The stall was made of fancy stones and tiles, a half wall of smooth rocks keeping the stream from flooding the floor and providing scant privacy. It even had two corner seats made from teak. Joe had some funky organic body wash that smelled like mangoes mixed with clove and musk. Malachi made a face at the scent, but scrubbed from head to toe, letting the warm water work the kinks from his neck and shoulders. Kissing Mia replayed in his mind, and Mr. Woody stood at attention, begging for release.

He braced his hands on the stone shower stall, bowing and letting the spray run down his back. He was a trained endurance athlete. He could go for miles, hours, on nothing but willpower, controlling his body and mind. But for the life of him, he couldn't control his dick when she was near.

He sighed, regarded his erection, willing it to deflate. Fat chance, that.

Movement from the corner of his eye made him jump, instantly in soldier-mode and ready for an attack.

The threat stole his breath away. Mia, as naked as her fantasy self in his mental movie, stood watching him. The stone wall was the only thing between them and he had to blink a couple times as he took her all in. Was he losing it? Dreaming? Had his imagination taken over?

She gave him that barely-there smile—unsure, shy. A scar ran from one shoulder down her arm. Another left a thin pale line across her ribs. More crisscrossed her thighs. This was no mirage, no fantasy.

Anger rose inside him, and he steamed hotter than the water. Her eyes roamed over his upper body, pausing on the scar and corresponding tattoo on his left pec. He'd been shot in Afghanistan during the mission that had changed Caleb forever. Malachi had added the tat to honor that assignment and at the same time, change the scar from an ugly reminder of that day into a striking phoenix, rising from the ashes.

Studying it, something changed in her eyes. He'd witnessed it before in other survivors—camaraderie. "I don't usually do this kind of thing." She spoke over the sound of the water, her voice husky, hesitant. "I've known you for less than twenty-four hours, and well, if you haven't guessed, my life is really screwed up. I'm screwed up. If you want me to leave, I will. I totally get it. I'm being presumptuous, but—"

He left the shower and cut her off, grabbing her and kissing her. She wrapped her arms around his neck, pressed her generous breasts into him. Her stomach teased his erection, and she came up on her toes.

She was vulnerable. He felt like a cad to take advantage of it. Breaking the kiss, his breath coming hard, he put space between them. "Turn around."

A flash of panic flared in her eyes. "Why?"

"I want to see all of you."

Slowly, she lowered her gaze, studied his dick, then pivoted on bare feet to expose her back. As he suspected, more scars laced her shoulders, her spine. He wanted to hit something, kill someone.

The culprit was already dead. All Malachi could do now was take her pain away.

He moved in and held her close, his front to her backside. Her head dipped, and he sensed again how vulnerable she felt. He stroked her hair, shifting it, and lowering his mouth to her ear. "Technically, it's been twenty-eight hours since our initial meeting, and we've lived weeks—years—in that time."

She relaxed into him, sighing. "True, but just so you know, I've never felt like this about anyone."

He nibbled her earlobe, ran his teeth down her neck. Gently bit her shoulder. "It's the same for me. I promise, I'll never hurt you."

Her breath hitched. Her throat bobbed as she swallowed and laid her head against his shoulder, exposing her throat. "I know you won't."

He cupped her breasts and massaged the glorious mounds, continuing to trail his lips over her skin. Her nipples grew hard, and she arched as he sent one hand lower to the apex of her thighs.

"Oooh," she murmured as he cupped her. She was slick and ready for his probing fingers, shifting her legs apart and pressing her butt into his cock, egging him on. Within a few strokes, she was begging him for more.

He smiled, happy to oblige.

He didn't want to rush one minute of it though, so he eased out of her, ignoring her whimpers of protest, and bent to kiss the scars on her back. As his lips touched the first, she gasped and started to pull away. He held her hips, continuing, one by one, to use his mouth to worship the marks.

Kissing and licking at them caused her resistance to fade. He turned her to face him, watching her expression of bliss, as he repeated the process on her front, moving over her shoulder, her ribs, pausing at each breast to suck the dark areoles into his mouth and venerate them as well.

She clutched his shoulders, and when he went lower to her shapely thighs, her fingers sank into his hair. She held on tight.

He brought his mouth to her tender, sensitive flesh, and she orgasmed instantly, crying his name. Using his tongue and fingers, he stroked her, teasing it out. He especially loved it when she cut loose and swore a blue streak at the peak of her climax.

She went limp in his arms. Something fell from her left hand, and he saw a condom on the floor. He held her and when she could breathe, she said, "I found it in the closet drawer. Do you think Joe and Sam will mind?"

A chuckle rose from his chest. "Condoms are sometimes used for protecting small electronics and gadgets from moisture and sand when undercover. Trust me, I'm happy to buy Joe a new supply if Sam wants a replacement."

"Oh good." She sagged, her legs weak. "There's plenty more if we need them."

He loved her in that moment. Picking up the packet, he made a promise to himself that they most certainly would need the entire box.

Carrying her into the shower, he sat her on one of the corner benches. Tearing the wrapper open, he started to put the condom on. Mia crooked a finger at him. "Can I do the honors?"

Erection bobbing happily, he returned to her. She took it, and palmed him, circling her fingers around his length with a solid grip. She lowered her head, and *bam*, he did his own cursing when her warm mouth sucked him in.

Once more, he braced his hands, but this time, he let go of his control. As she built her rhythm, he murmured her name, stroking her hair. A second before he went over the edge, he forced himself to stop her. Her eyes were emeralds again in the dim light, her breathing as fast as his. With trembling hands, she rolled the latex on and then put her arms on his shoulders, as he lifted her up and pressed her against the wall.

Her amazing legs tangled around his hips, and they fit perfectly together. One of her hands guided him in and everything slowed to this single moment of connection.

"Thank you," she murmured and closed her eyes.

"Look at me." His voice was low, rough, echoing off the tiles. "I want to see your eyes as we do this."

She obeyed, pinning those beautiful green orbs on him. Her expression sent a ripple down his spine. "Why?"

"Because that's where the truth lies." One of these days, he needed to confess about the guilt he carried for not catching Lopez and stopping him from kidnapping her. While that wasn't now, he wanted her to see he felt the same way she did. *Soon. I'll tell her later today.* "You're sure about this?" he asked.

Her answer was to kiss him, hot, heavy, lots of tongue. "For the first time since this all happened," she told him, "I'm absolutely positive this is what I want."

Malachi held her gaze, losing himself in it, and plunged inside her. As she gasped, he gave her a moment to adjust to his size. The signal that she was ready came with a rock of her hips, drawing him in deeper.

Together they built a steady rhythm. She kept closing her eyes, riding the building waves, and he kept demanding that she open them. They worshipped their connection, giving it their all, and enjoying the building tension. He murmured words of encouragement, telling her how amazing she was, how much he wanted her.

He felt her climax squeeze him tightly as he sucked at her bottom lip. "Come on, Mia. Give me everything." He drove deeper, relishing her moan of desire. "Let go. I'll catch you."

With a thrust of her hips, she cried, bucking against him hard. Over and over, she slammed him home, as she spasmed around his cock. He rode it with her, gritting his teeth until she was done and boneless in his arms. Still, she kept her blissed out gaze on him and her nails dug into his shoulders. "Who says you can't find the man of your dreams at the library?"

His ears were buzzing, her words so soft he wasn't sure he'd heard her over the fall of the water. "What?"

"Nothing." She gave him a wicked grin and another hip thrust. "Your turn."

He kissed her and in two more swift thrusts, he couldn't hold back any longer. He came in a blinding rush, the endurance he was so proud of, that he'd worked so hard to gain, gone in the flick of her tongue, the feel of her coming again under him.

It was so worth it.

For long moments they stood suspended, alone but with each other, lost in oblivion. In the silence that followed, she clung to him and he to her. Survivors learning to live again.

When his breath returned to semi-normal, he shifted them, and on strong legs, disposed of the condom and began washing her.

FIFTEEN

Cooper rubbed his tired eyes and chomped on a carrot stick. The words on the papers in front of him blurred.

"Why don't you take a break?" Celina slid a cold beer toward him. "Play with Nova while I draw her bath."

Owen played peekaboo with his baby sister in the living room, Nova's toddler squeals making Cooper smile. His son, looking more like a young man every day, ducked behind the couch, then popped up to Nova's delight. She clapped her chubby hands and cried, "Do it again, Wenny!"

Thunder, the resident Chihuahua, barked his agreement. Cooper kicked back in the dining room chair and tossed the remains of the carrot onto a plate. He enjoyed a long sip, then lowered his voice. "Clock's ticking on this. We could have a dead mayor by morning."

Celina watched as Owen did as commanded, making the toddler happy. She spoke softly as well. "If they wanted her dead, why not execute her last night? Why kidnap her?"

"None of this makes sense, no matter how many times I pore through the reports."

"You're tired, and I'm sure your eyes need a rest."

He studied them again, attempting to bring the words into focus. It didn't work. Damn carrots. They were supposed to strengthen your sight, but so far, they'd done nothing for his.

"You know, getting reading glasses is nothing to be ashamed of," Celina told him firmly. "Dr. Betting said it's normal in your forties to need them."

Never one to beat around the bush, she had to bring up his age. "I don't."

"How about a magnifying glass? I have one in my camera bag." Her grin was pure evil, her dark eyes flashing with humor. "I can call you Sherlock."

"Laugh all you want. Eventually, you'll be at this stage and the tables will be turned." He'd probably be headed for adult diapers by then, due to their age difference, but he had a memory like an elephant. "Oh, who am I kidding? You'll be just as gorgeous with glasses and gray hair, while I'll just be... old."

She rose from her seat and came to lean over his back, wrapping her arms around his neck and letting her fingers tickle his chest. "You're not old, and you're still the sexiest man I've ever seen. Glasses are hot—you looked even sexier with them. And,"—she flicked the end of her tongue across the ridge of his ear and whispered—"you'll be able to see everything, including minute details, of the things I plan to do to you, once you have a pair."

Owen ran off down the hall toward the bedrooms, and Nova's chubby legs followed, bare feet slapping the tile floor. Thunder followed, determined not to be left out.

Cooper's dick responded to his wife's words and the tongue that traced down his neck. "Is that so?"

"I can find more interesting things than carrots to feed you."

He sighed and pulled her to his lap. "I'll consider the glasses. Getting old sucks."

She kissed him. "You're virile, strong, and hot as ever. What about any of that sucks?"

His ego responded to her flattery, just like always. "You deserve better."

"I don't want anyone but you, never have and never will."

He kissed her and they made out for a few minutes, the sound of their happy children in the background. She wanted more kids, and Cooper wanted her to be happy. He worried his job wasn't conducive to family life, but they'd made it work so far, and hell, you only lived once, right?

His cell rang and Celina broke away. She was breathing heavy and her eyes were dark chocolate. "Duty calls."

Before he could argue, she slipped from him, dropping a kiss on his forehead. Her hips swayed as he watched, taunting him in her skin tight yoga pants. "But we'll pick this up again later," she said over her shoulder with a wink.

He grinned, watching her until she disappeared.

It was Thomas on the phone.

"Tell me you got something," Cooper said.

"I've talked to a dozen snitches and tried everything I know to uncover a lead. I've got nada. It doesn't add up, Coop. Not the mayor's kidnapping, not Mia's last year either. It's like a maze and we can see all these different paths, but we can't see the center. A huge chunk of this puzzle is hidden. The leads we have are slim or utter dead ends, yet they are all connected to these two sisters."

Cooper shoved the plate out of the way. "We just have to hope the SWAT team finds Amber and arrests those responsible."

A long silence descended, and Cooper could hear the cogs in Thomas's brain turning. He hadn't been the same since his last undercover mission. He'd been held against his will and tortured nearly to the brink of death. He'd lost his lighthearted banter, and never spouted movie quotes anymore. Cooper suspected he was taking this case more personally than most because it hit close to home. "Damon Marcher was a businessman," Thomas said. "What made him step down from that loft, where he never got his hands dirty, to torture Mia Livingston? It's out of character."

Cooper turned the beer bottle in circles. "He wanted to force the mayor's hand, show her he had power over her."

"A blackmailer like him doesn't turn to kidnapping without a strong motive. Marcher always stayed behind the scenes, a puppet master. Surely there were more effective ways to put pressure on the mayor without putting himself under fire."

"I get that, but unless this line of analysis is going to help us locate her, you might as well stop spinning your wheels."

"Noted, but..."

Cooper waited, taking a drink. When Thomas didn't continue, he prompted him. "Spit it out, Mann. But what?"

"Nothing. Just thinking of ways to find her."

"And?"

"In the video, the guy told Mia he'd come back for her. She could be the thread that leads to the center of the maze."

Cooper had come from the DEA. Some days, he thought about going back. Problem was, he loved the SCVC Taskforce, and while drug dealers tended to be easier to understand, and therefore flush out, these types of cases challenged him and his team to go deeper. "Dupé will never go for using her as a lure. Keep at it with your connections. Someone has to know something. Meantime, I have another idea. Remember when Bianca was with us? Her friend, what was his name? He had that software program that could figure out random connections between people."

"Emit Petit?"

"That's him. Maybe she can feed all these random names, dates, and places into that program to get something more solid for us."

The sound of an engine could be heard in the background. Thomas was heading somewhere. "Worth a try. Just remember, she's Beatrice now."

An NSA brainiac who'd once been part of his team, she had changed her identity and relocated to the East Coast after an assassin had come after her. She hadn't, however, gone into hiding. In fact, she and her husband, Cal, had started a security business, hiring former SEALs who struggled to find jobs aligned with their skill set. Rumor had it their teams also performed certain paramilitary missions, serving up justice wherever they went. "Has Ronni gone through the mayor's correspondence?"

"Still working on it. By the way, sounds like the mayor had the city council in an uproar about a hiring vacancy for the finance department. That woman who was embezzling and got sent to jail last year—they've never filled that position because the mayor won't sign off on who the council wants. Pissed them off, I guess, but doesn't seem like a reason to have her taken, does it?"

Thomas was thinking outside the box, toying with other possibilities besides the former Quattro Gang looking for revenge. It was definitely a good idea, but city council members seemed an unlikely lot to have done this.

Cooper hated politics, and couldn't imagine holding office. Even Dupé's position was rife with drama and malcontents. He checked his watch. "Let me get this call into Bian—I mean, *Beatrice*—and then we'll walk through everything at the office. Tell Bobby and the others to meet us there, and include the Cahills."

"What about Mia?"

Cooper thought about it. "I'm sure she's with Malachi, so we don't have much choice, although Sam is pretty sure he took the bait. They're probably checking the spot the SWAT team is raiding soon."

"Cahill will be pissed if he realizes you kept him busy chasing his tail."

Cooper leaned back and smiled. "He should've followed my orders yesterday, and I know he'll defy any others I give him. That location is solid and it *is* a possibility Amber is there. A slim one, I know, but I couldn't simply hand him the address —Dupé would kill me if he found out. It was the best I could do to send him and Mia in that direction."

"You're not Cahill's boss, Coop."

Down the hall, Nova squealed with delight. He could hear Celina chasing her, ordering her to the tub. "True, but you don't mess with the Beast. Keep an eye on him, will you? Cross your fingers our analysis is right and we get our mayor back in one piece. Soon."

"Time is working against us."

"All the more reason to get a fresh set of eyes on this."

"Meet you at the office." Thomas disconnected.

Cooper's next call went to a private number and a man answered. "Rockstar Security. How may I help you?"

"I need to speak with Beatrice."

A pause. "Are you in need of protection?"

"I am in need of you putting me through to your boss. Tell her the Beast is calling. Trust me, she'll take it."

Another pause, this more resistant, as though a wall had gone up between them. "One moment."

The line played a classic rock song, and a minute later, a familiar voice came on. "What do I owe this unexpected call to? Is Celina okay?"

She knew him well. Celina and the kids were everything to him. He never asked for help, but for them, he'd do anything, including beg, borrow, and steal. "The family is good. Yours?"

He heard her take a small, relieved breath. "We are well, also. I take it this isn't a social call."

"The Taskforce has an emergency."

"I've seen the news. Is this about the mayor?"

"Yes. We don't have motivation, culprits, or any strong leads. SWAT is raiding our best guess tonight, but I've got a bad feeling about this whole thing. If she's not there, we're sunk."

"How can I help?"

"We have too many loose ends and no clear connections. If I send you a list of names, dates, and places, can you use Petit's program to find the piece of this puzzle that I'm missing?"

She was silent for a heartbeat. "The software is proprietary and Emit doesn't like using it for government purposes."

Cooper dug in his heels. "I wouldn't ask if this woman's life wasn't on the line."

Beatrice had a genius IQ and complete recall for anything she'd seen, heard, or read. The thought of all that data in one brain made his head hurt. "You know I am indebted to you, but the government has caused Cal and myself a great deal of grief. We've found that loaning out our software leads to conflict between us and, well, you."

He knew she meant the collective law enforcement 'you.' It still rankled.

She was stubborn, but so was he. "I'll keep it off the record. Nobody will know, even if you find a valid link that helps us. I'm desperate, B."

A noise in the background filtered through and he heard Cal's voice. Beatrice covered the receiver and they had a brief conversation. "Fine," she said, reluctantly, when she returned to the line. "Send me the information at this email." She rattled it off. "I'll do this one time, under anonymity, and you'll owe us."

It was a fair deal. Celina appeared with Nova wrapped in a towel. She brought the wiggling, wet child over, and he kissed her fresh smelling head.

She patted his cheeks. "Night, Dada."

"Night, baby girl," he said to her, and then to Beatrice, "Thank you. I appreciate it more than you know."

"Come for a visit." He heard her typing. "We'd love to get Nova and Sloane together for a playdate."

"The road goes both ways, and so does the offer. Plus, the weather's better here," he teased.

"Good to talk to you, Beast." The line went dead

Celina stepped back and Nova looked around for Owen and Thunder. "Who was that?"

"Beatrice Reese." He wrapped both his girls in his arms and kissed them.

Nova laughed and Celina gave him the stink eye, as he began gathering the papers. "You're leaving?"

"Raincheck on our plans for later?"

She huffed, but without real effort. "Did you get a lead?"

"Working on it." He stuck the papers in his briefcase and headed for the door. "I'll check in with you as soon as I can, but don't wait up."

Pinching her lips, she followed him. "Good luck. I hope you find her."

He gave her another kiss. "Me, too." The night was chilly and stark as he stepped outside. "We've got to."

SIXTEEN

Mia's body felt flush and alive for the first time in months. Her nerves buzzed pleasantly in the continuing afterglow of Malachi's lovemaking and her brain felt clearer, sharper.

The ocean was dark, a cloudy night sky accompanying them as they took the coastal highway south back to San Diego.

Her disguise was more like camouflage, and the bulletproof vest Malachi insisted she wear added bulk and weight to her torso. Her boobs felt squished, but he wouldn't have let her come unless she followed all his rules. Wearing it was one of them.

She worried her hands in her lap, the dark gloves he'd given her ready if she needed them. The landscape around the former lab's compound had appeared to be overgrown, and he insisted she wear thick-soled boots with long pants and sleeves to protect her skin.

She didn't believe he'd let her get out of his truck once they arrived, but he had prepped her for any and all contingencies.

She liked that about him. For once, it was nice to lean on

someone else when it came to overthinking the possible threats that lay in the dark.

A strand of black hair tickled her chin. She tucked it behind her ear. The wig was high quality and light on her skull but still felt odd, itchy. As he'd dressed her, he'd questioned her on various things—the night Lopez had grabbed her outside the fundraiser, the things Marcher had said to her, did Amber have any enemies? Usually, recounting her ordeal was fresh torture, but this time, she'd felt a healthy detachment, as though it hadn't all happened to her.

Probably still riding the high from his touch, his kiss. She didn't want to come down from that, and certainly not to relive her ordeal.

Underneath it all, she sensed he was getting at something. Laying out all the events, the tiny details, like a general preparing for battle. The questions were leading him down a path. He'd thought over each of her responses, asked more, then frowned in consternation at a few of her answers. She'd chuckled at the question about Amber's enemies—didn't every politician have plenty of those? But Malachi had wanted to know about non-work ones—friends, family, boyfriends, or donors whom she might have had closer relationships with that could have been upset with her over personal things. There was a handful of exes, but Mia couldn't see any of them as threats. There was Constance—Amber's college roommate who'd been her finance manager. Amber had given her a job with the city when she'd been elected, only, Constance had been embezzling from the campaign funds, and Amber had been horrified. Pressing charges and sending her friend to jail had taken a toll on Amber, but Constance was no threat now.

Besides, Mia was sure this was King and Lopez, not an unhappy ex, behind her sister's kidnapping. Those two were playing a game to get at Newt Marcher.

Malachi took a turn, leaving the highway. "You're quiet. You okay?"

She bit her bottom lip. They'd left Ladybug at Mia's apartment. The lack of her constant companion was as odd as wearing the vest and wig. "Just trying to figure out, still, why these men took my sister and where she could be. I feel like we're spinning our wheels."

"I know this is tough, but remember, everyone is doing their best to find her."

But don't get your hopes up.

The unsaid words hung between them. She took a slow, steadying breath. The tone in his voice was a familiar one. "Are you prepping me for disappointment?"

He glanced at her. "She may not be there. Odds are she isn't. There are hundreds of places they could have taken her."

"You don't excel at pep talks, do you?" Mia had spoken to her parents before they'd left. Her mother was convinced and hopeful that a ransom call would come. They had no money to speak of, so it would be pointless to demand they pay up, but Mia had played along. This raid had to work. They had to find Amber and bring her home.

Malachi chuckled without humor. "I'm better at giving orders."

"I noticed," she teased. She reached over and caught his hand, threading her fingers through his. "Thank you for doing this. For defying Dupé and bringing me to the takedown."

His strong fingers closed around hers. "If they see us, my ass is grass. We have to remain outside the perimeters and lay low."

"I know, but it means a lot to me that you would risk your good standing with the Taskforce to let me be here."

"I owe you that much."

What an odd thing to say. "You don't owe me anything."

His eyes stayed locked on the road. Lights from oncoming traffic rolled over his features. "Mia, there's something I've been meaning to tell you—"

His phone rang, echoing in the cab. The truck's navigation system was paired with it, and the screen lit up with the caller ID—C Harris.

Another ring, and Mia glanced at Malachi. "Do you want me to answer it?"

He shook his head, released her hand, and pressed the connect button. "What's up?"

Harris sounded annoyed. "Did you get Thomas's message?"

"I did."

"Are you planning on gracing us with your presence sometime before Christmas?"

Malachi laughed easily. Then he lied just as easily. "We're on our way. Got caught up in some traffic. Must be important if you want us there in person."

Harris continued to sound gruff, but Mia decided that was his norm. "I need to ask Mia more questions. What's your ETA?"

She looked questioningly at Malachi. He hadn't said anything about Thomas telling him to come to the office.

He didn't look her way, keeping his focus on the road. As they made another turn, heading into an industrial area, he continued with his ruse. "Shouldn't be much longer. Any chance you can ask her these pressing things over the phone?"

"No," the Taskforce leader said. "By the way, they went to pick up King tonight, and he's slipped his tracker. He's in the wind. You need to be extra careful. He might come after Mia."

Her stomach dropped.

The road became narrower with far less traffic. Malachi

smacked the steering wheel. "Dupé should have never agreed to this deal in the first place."

Harris ruminated for a moment and then said, "Agreed, but that doesn't change the current situation."

Another turn, and she saw a sign warning about private property. Malachi sped past it. "Tell me you have a plan to find him."

A sign, half blown over, announced the landfill up ahead. Malachi pulled off and drove down a sandy side street.

"Law enforcement is on it," Harris replied.

They wheeled behind a dilapidated building. The place looked like a metal works shop. As the headlights bounced from the rutted out road, they flashed off metal fencing. "That won't be enough," Malachi grumbled.

Most of the fence was covered by vines and climbing weeds. Scrub palms and cacti intermingled with the brush along the perimeter.

"No it won't," Harris said. "Which is why I have the go ahead from Dupé to officially hire Bondsmen Brothers to track down our fugitive."

Malachi appeared unimpressed, parking behind the largest structure. He sat there a moment, that same intelligent expression on his face, as when he questioned her earlier. "Joe will handle the paperwork. See you in a few." He disconnected before Harris could say anything else.

Mia pointed to the clock. "It's almost time."

His phone rang again. This time it was Caleb's name that popped up. Malachi hit the connect button again. "What have you got for me, bro?"

"Something you need to look at. Sending the photo now."

A ping came from the phone, and Malachi opened a text. "Leandro Lopez. What about him? Is the guy next to him our friend from last night?"

"I think they're one and the same. I had Bobby use a software program to remove Lopez's beard and then put scars on his cheeks. You're looking at him, Mal."

Mia grabbed the phone, eyeing the two faces that were side by side in the picture. The angled jawlines were a match, and the expanse of neck under them, complete with a mole, was what she'd seen last night when the half-masked man had threatened her. "But Lopez is Latino, isn't he?"

Caleb sounded slightly amped as he explained. "Josie and I were cross-referencing everyone associated with the case, and she found images on social media that raised a few interesting questions. Group shots at one of our mayor's fundraisers, shortly after she took office. Both Jam King and this guy, without the beard and mustache, are in the background of two. I ran his face through our database but came up with jack. Bobby, however, got a hit on Interpol. Don't ask me how he can access their databases, I'm sure I don't want to know. Oh hell, of course I do, and I'm gonna make him show me, but for now, anyway, meet Josip Horvat."

"Who the hell is that?" Malachi asked.

"A Croatian national specializing in extortion and a host of other crimes, like kidnapping and blackmail. He broke out of prison over there six years ago, thanks to a man linked to a Korean mafia, and apparently he went underground only to reappear here in the States."

"A new identity, but the same bag of tricks," Malachi murmured. "I bet he and Marcher hit it off big."

"Plus, it's our missing link with Komosu. According to Interpol, he's fluent in languages besides English— Spanish, Russian, Korean and German. Dad was Croatian, but mom was from Mexico."

"That bastard. He's eluded everyone right from the start."

Malachi punched the dash. "We need to run him down once and for all."

"Here's the other interesting thing," Caleb continued. "The social media posts? They were by a woman who worked for the mayor, a Constance Cronenworth. She was the gal—"

"Who embezzled from Amber," Mia cut in, surprised and angry all at the same time. "She and my sister were close, so it's not surprising she shared photos of those parties, but..."

"But what were King and Lopez— Horvat—doing there?" Caleb finished for her.

Malachi glanced at her. "They were already planning something then."

She struggled to think back, searching her memories for either of them. "There were so many events and fundraisers, I don't remember them all. I certainly don't recall seeing either man at any of them."

"When I was crosschecking Cronenworth with their names," Caleb said, "King was listed as a visitor on the prison logs last March, only a few days after Constance arrived. He visited her several times that month, but then never again."

Mia gripped the seat. "She was in cahoots with them?"

"We're doing more digging," Caleb assured her. "But there's definitely more to this than we previously realized."

Malachi drummed his fingers on the steering wheel, his gaze not on the night outside the windshield, but somewhere else entirely. "The Feds should have caught this. I need to question Cronenworth. ASAP." He killed the engine causing the darkness to settle in around them. "Also I have the distinct impression we've been misled about this raid."

"What do you mean?" Mia asked.

Malachi looked ready to explode. "Don't tell the Taskforce about the connection you found to Cronenworth yet," he instructed his brother. "See how fast you can get me in to see her."

Caleb sounded less than excited about that prospect. "Withholding information—"

Malachi cut him off. "Isn't smart, I know. No lectures. They're holding out on us, too."

Mia leaned toward him, trying to catch his eye. "Malachi, please tell me what's going on."

Just then a group of three black sprinter vans sped by, lights off and kicking up dust as they zoomed down the road.

"Hold on." Malachi dimmed the dash lights and picked up the phone. "Maybe I was wrong—looks like something is going down. Arrange at least a phone call with that woman, bro, and tell Joe to pull strings if need be, but tell anyone who asks that I'm out of the loop for now."

"I don't think that's a good idea, and not just because Sam will take it from all of our hides,' Caleb argued.

"I don't know if it's Dupé, the Taskforce, or the Bureau in general who are playing games, but they are. Besides that, they move too damn slow." Malachi started checking his pockets. "The info they get is always old and it places us behind the eight ball. If we're going to get ahead of King and Horvat, we have to move quicker than they do. It's time to shake some cages."

Caleb's sigh was audible. "I'm the first to rebel against the establishment, and far be it from me to criticize your unexpected insurrection, but it's really not like you, Mal."

Malachi zipped his vest. "Gotta go. Text me when you've got the meeting set up."

He disconnected, grabbing a flashlight and handing it to Mia, along with a pair of goggles. Next, he donned a windbreaker from the backseat and she noticed its pockets were full of more gear. "Sit tight," he told her. He checked his gun and reholstered it. "I'll do a perimeter scan and return once I ascertain what's going down. Do not leave the vehicle. I will come back for you."

Her blood racing and a dozen questions tugging at her brain, she leaned across the console and kissed him. "For Amber," she said.

"For Amber," he replied.

SEVENTEEN

Malachi hated leaving Mia, but he had no idea what he was walking into. Safer to retrieve her and go back once he was sure they could observe the takedown—if there was one. He prayed that Amber was here, that they could rescue her tonight, but his gut told him that was too easy.

His night vision goggles showed him a greenish panorama filled with palm trees, vines, and scrub brush left to Mother Nature's whims. He trudged through sand and weeds, the pant legs he'd tucked into his boots catching on the razor-sharp points of various cacti and succulents.

Far off in the distance, a coyote bayed, the lonely sound adding a macabre eeriness on the arid night air. Afghanistan had been similar to this. Long nights spent in the desert, an oasis here and there with clumps of nomads, barely surviving the terrain. There he'd worried about IEDs, enemy gunfire, ambushes. Here, it was a landfill—potentially used for body disposal—a lab where ricin had toxified the ground for a time. The night was still, yet a variety of odors rode the air—rotting things all mixed together in the landfill's soup.

He skirted the western edge of the dump, making his way toward the laboratory grounds. The fence around it had more than one breach point where animals or fallen branches had managed to create a hole. Near a stand of what appeared to be fruit trees, an entire section had been torn down. Things moved in the night around him, snakes and various rodents, but he kept his focus on finding a vantage point to watch the SWAT team.

He was on them in seconds, the sound of bodies nearby made him pause. They weren't noisy, but his ears were highly sensitive, thanks to his training. He wasn't able to see the main entrance to the lab, but he could make out the rear platform. He kept going, carefully, deliberately, until the SWAT vans were a dim outline in their hidden spots along the drive.

Continuing on, he saw the team staking out the area, moving with guns and purpose.

The rush of adrenaline hit him hard. This was a foolish risk, especially if Harris and Sam hadn't deceived him. Amber Livingston might well be in that building, and if her captors were with her, things could go sideways fast.

Unlike Caleb, he rarely took this kind of chance unless it was well calculated. But tonight, he had to do it for Mia.

He needed a better vantage point and wondered how much time he had before they breached the place. Calculated risk—that's what she was for him. He'd never fallen for anyone this hard, this fast, and she was bound to leave him in the dust when this was over. She'd sought refuge with him because he'd offered hope, a lifeline during this crisis. It was normal human behavior, and he didn't begrudge her that. Hell, he'd let her take advantage of him anywhere, anytime.

Only...he found he wanted more. He didn't want to be her temporary lifeline. He'd found himself in her eyes. Renewed his love of life by helping her find hers.

Damn, he had it bad. He'd never been one for mere infatuations or one-night stands. He liked stability, someone to come home to. The long-haul—that's what he wanted.

And didn't that scare the ever-loving hell out of him? First Joe, then Caleb. *What are the odds I get Mia and a dog?*

Moving on silent feet, he kept a wide berth between him and the others, a tiny smile refusing to stay off his face. He tried to refocus, stop thinking about Mia and the future, and get his head on straight. He'd thought about going into SWAT at one point after he left the Marines. He had the skills, willpower and determination. A close friend, a sniper in his unit, had joined the FBI 'enhanced' team not long ago. He hadn't spoken to Norrie in months. He might be here tonight. On the north side, he spotted a two-story metal warehouse. Most of the windows were broken, and it appeared as though a fire had burned a section of it. The ground it sat on rose slightly and butted up to the landfill's westernmost ditch. If he and Mia could find a lookout there, they could see the side of the lab, along with both front and back exits.

As he made his decision to double back and get her, he noted the loading dock had a large, rectangular delivery truck next to it. Dirty and rundown, the sides bore a business logo that had been weathered away. Was that what Marcher had used to transport her? He had more questions than answers, and it bugged the shit out of him.

Retracing his steps through the overgrown wall of vegetation, his mind flashed to his desert tours again. The nomadic farmers moved their tiny, scrawny herds from one watering hole to another, seeking food and survival for the animals who were worth more than gold. Sometimes, they had no fixed home, taking their families with them, staying away from the fighting, and attempting to disappear in order to stay alive.

Marcher had been paranoid, had known the depth of

trouble he'd landed in, and had probably moved Mia to keep one step ahead of the cops.

Malachi barely avoided a snake coiled near a fallen stump. The thing jolted at his sudden appearance, then slithered away under a palmetto. *Focus*, he reminded himself.

But it didn't make sense. In many ways, Damon Marcher understood calculated risk the same as Malachi did. Why would he have put his international empire, and his life, at risk by kidnapping Mia?

It's personal. The surety beat at his brain.

There seemed to be a lot Amber hadn't shared with Mia. Could she have been involved with Marcher somehow? No, the Feds would have discovered any relationship if they'd had one.

Then what? Seemed Marcher's actions had been triggered by something more than manipulating the mayor to do what he wanted.

But then again, Mia had told him about the man's ramblings. To her, he'd seemed unhinged, disturbed. He'd definitely become unstable.

Taking her hostage had been a foolish endeavor and he had to have known it. Malachi would bet his dusty boots it had something to do with Constance Cronenworth. But what? Had she been a girlfriend, a sister?

The truck came into view. Seeing him, Mia flew out of the passenger side and into his arms. He hugged her tight, setting her on her feet a few inches from him.

"Is she there?" She teetered on the knife-edge of joy and disappointment.

"I don't know," he told her. "There's no activity inside I can see. No vehicles, other than SWAT and a broken-down panel van."

She deflated. "So probably not."

Probably not, but it was possible that some small detail of

the place would spark her memory if she'd been held there. It was a long shot, but he'd been around enough men and women with PTSD, and he understood what trauma could do to a person. The brain and heart liked to close off specific memories to protect you. What might seem inconsequential could bring forth a thought that could evoke a revelation. He was no expert, no psychologist, but it didn't take one to realize Mia had a lot of healing yet to do.

Taking a stun stick the size of a Maglite from his pant pocket, he showed her how it worked.

"Wow," she said, flinching at the electrical buzz that resonated from the double prongs. "That makes my version look like a wimp."

He held out a hand. "Ready? Don't hesitate to use it if you need to."

She slid her hand into his, lowering her goggles before accepting the weapon. "I'm more than ready."

Now familiar with the path, he hustled her to the lab.

EIGHTEEN

Mia wasn't a runner and their trek seemed like an obstacle course. Her legs had trouble keeping up with Malachi's, although she admired his athleticism. She tripped once, nearly losing the stun stick, the night vision goggles messing with her depth perception. Malachi didn't say a word, simply helped her stand and pushed on.

They had entered a deserted building that smelled like garbage and made her gag when they heard a commotion coming from the direction of the lab. "Go!" Malachi pointed toward a set of metal stairs leading up to the second floor.

Adrenaline offering a burst of speed, she took them two at a time. He followed and urged her to a lookout position at a dusty, broken window.

Bats descended from perches above, causing Mia to nearly scream as tiny wings flapped near her head. She waved the stun gun to fend them off and felt Malachi grip her wrist, holding the weapon at bay. It was only then that she realized she'd nearly clobbered him with her knee-jerk reaction.

He tugged her gently in front of him, pointing out the hole

of the busted glass. She caught the soft chatter of radios, and instinctively turned her ear toward them, holding her breath to listen.

The SWAT team moved like nocturnal creatures, flowing into the building quickly in a long chain. Malachi silently indicated several stationed outside as well, and another chain entering at the rear.

Her stomach tensed, seeing the loading dock and the dirty panel truck, dirty and bluish-white in the moonlight. Something in the recesses of her memory twinged. "Do you think Damon was bringing me here to kill me that night?"

Malachi's breath was warm on her neck. "What?"

Anxiety cramped inside her chest. Her breathing grew shaky and she knew it wasn't from the effects of hurrying through the woods. "When he was caught. Sam said we were only a few miles from here." Her teeth chattered, and her limbs trembled. "He was going to kill me and cremate my body or toss it in the landfill, wasn't he?"

Malachi's arms went around her. "You're safe now."

It wasn't confirmation, and yet it was. She truly had been close to death that night.

Staring at the lab, she wondered if she'd been inside it, like Sam had suggested. Did it have a holding cell? Was Amber in there now?

She closed her eyes and forced her breathing to slow. Reliving old memories or speculating about what might have happened did no one any good. Being here for Amber, if she needed her, would.

Minutes felt like hours as they watched. Voices floated to them as the SWAT team members called out.

"What's taking so long?" she asked. "Do you think they found her?"

Malachi's chest, with its layers and pockets filled with

various items, heaved on a tight sigh. "We'd know if they had encountered anyone, especially Amber. King and Lopez—Horvat—would not leave her unguarded."

He'd told her it would be a long shot, and he'd been right. "What about the other sites? Maybe we should try them?"

"I haven't heard anything yet, and we'd know if they'd found something. Sam would call."

"You told Caleb you thought we'd been misled—did you mean by her? Why would she do that?"

"To keep you safe. It's no surprise you'd demand to be here when the unit went in. They wanted to keep us both out of the way."

Several men returned outside, and numerous radio discussions took place. They fanned out and began a sweep of the terrain.

Malachi tugged her from the window, drawing out binoculars. "I'm sorry, but it looks like this was a bust."

Renewed anger and frustration boiled under her skin. "How did you know?"

"Know what?"

"That they didn't really think she was here?"

He glanced through the lenses, keeping an eye on those who might come their direction. Then he lowered them and a slice of moonlight danced across his face, making his blue irises turn icy. "Did you see any of the Taskforce here?"

"No."

"I got that call from Harris right before this went down. Do you really think he and his team would sit at their office if they believed Amber was here?"

She hadn't thought of that. "So they figured there was a possibility and covered their asses by sending SWAT, but since the chances were slim, they stayed put to keep working."

He nodded.

"I wish everyone would stop trying to protect me. This is total bullshit, misleading us and getting my hopes up."

"I agree, but they think and act differently than you and me. They have systems and resources we can't touch, and layers of bureaucracy and red tape to go through. They see us as outsiders and ones who could get in the way, get hurt, or cause a mission to fail. We can't take it personally."

"Bullshit. I take this very personally."

She could tell he actually did, too, but realized that wasn't going to help.

He gave her arm a squeeze. "Would you rather be at their office going over details and analyzing the bad guys?"

She tilted her head slightly, thinking about it. "No."

He took her by the hand and led her out, avoiding the agents completing their search of the grounds. They gave the building a cursory sweep as Malachi and Mia stayed hidden yards from them, then they began to load up.

When they were finally leaving, Malachi guided her past the bushes. "Now we do our own inspection."

Her adrenaline surged as he flicked on his flashlight. She pocketed the stun gun, doing the same with hers.

"I noticed something earlier." He led her to the back of the lab. His beam slid over a section of ground near the loading dock, and she saw it flash off metal.

He stopped and bent down, using a gloved hand to brush debris from a metal door embedded in the ground. It had a handle and padlock.

"What is it?" Mia asked, shining her light on it as well.

"A door to a basement or a crawl space." The lock didn't give when he tugged on it. He tapped his fingers against it. "See anything odd about this?"

"You mean, other than there's a door in the ground?"

He smirked. "Look at the lock. The door is old and rusted, the handle pitted from sun and weather. But the lock..."

His meaning struck like a bolt of lightning. "It's new."

"It certainly hasn't been here long."

"We need to find out what's behind it," she said.

Malachi's phone must have vibrated. He reached into a pocket, checked the screen, and frowned. Then shoved it in and glanced at the door once more. He narrowed his eyes, his gaze catching on something next to it on the ground.

"Hello," he muttered and Mia saw what had caught his attention. He held it up to get a better look, and her legs went weak.

The glitter of gold flashed in the illumination from the beam, the twinkle of a diamond with it. Sensing her reaction, he held the earring toward her. "Do you recognize this?"

All she could do for a second was stare and hope her legs didn't give out. Swallowing hard, she found her voice. "It's Amber's."

"I'm on your left, Cahill," a familiar voice rang out. "Don't shoot, okay?"

A figure emerged from behind a tree. His hands were raised, a crowbar in one, and he blinked when she swung her light in his direction.

Malachi straightened, reaching for his gun, then barked, "What the hell, Mann?"

Thomas gave a lazy smile and motioned at Mia to lower her beam. She did, and he strode toward them, swinging the crowbar. "I called, but you didn't answer."

Malachi had dropped the jewelry and he bent to scoop it up once more. "Thought you were at the meeting."

Thomas glanced around as though bored. "I've found I don't have a lot of patience for them. I came here earlier, took a look around." He nudged his chin toward the metal door. "I see you found the entrance to whatever this place is hiding underground."

Mia took the earring and held it out to him. "This belongs to my sister. She bought them when she won the mayoral race. Could she be down there?"

Thomas handed Malachi the crowbar. "Put those big muscles of yours to work, Cahill, and let's find out."

NINETEEN

Thomas had long ago figured out he was similar to a cat—he had at least nine lives. He'd used quite a few of them in his line of work, and he owed a debt to the jerk in front of him for saving one of them a while back.

From the look on Cahill's face, he was regretting that rescue now.

Ronni had profiled the big oaf, and assured Coop the eldest Cahill was impeccable in word and deed. He was a strategic thinker, consistently toed the line, and got shit done. He was a classic overachiever and white knight, always saving others.

It had to be killing him not to be able to rescue Amber Livingston and make Mia happy. Thomas was doing what he could to help the guy, not only because of the debt, but because he liked him.

That meant dodging Coop and his orders, and he'd probably get a formal reprimand stuck in his file, but Thomas didn't really give a damn.

He held out the crowbar suspended between them, and yep, there it was—the guy eyed him as he accepted the makeshift weapon, tapping it in his palm twice before he went to work on the lock.

The white knight won over the renegade identity that Cahill was trying to embrace.

"I scanned the lab earlier," he told them both. "No traces of recent activity—no fresh blood stains or any sign of a struggle. Doesn't appear that the sinks or toilets have been used, no cigarette butts or trash visible. Still, it has the feel of..."

"What?" Malachi insisted.

"Someone's been here. They made sure not to leave a trail."

Mia cut her eyes between him and the lock, the crowbar screeching against the metal. "Of course they've been here. Amber's earring—"

"Good find." He nodded. "They may have come and gone in a hurry, and didn't use the interior. What I did notice is that the loading dock and the floor of the wing of the lab appear slightly higher than the rest, as if they were built into a hill, but they're not."

Under the brutal force of the crowbar, the lock popped and Cahill handed the bar back to Thomas. "No access inside to a basement or crawl space?"

"Not that I located, but my search wasn't thorough. I think this whole back area has a false floor." He noticed Mia's face light up. He didn't want to take that away, but he didn't think it fair to give her false optimism. "Even if there is, I doubt she's here."

"Why not?" Mia sounded pissed and she held out the earring. "She's obviously been here."

"They may have transferred her from one vehicle to another, or a guy got that hooked on a piece of clothing and dropped it here at some point after they kidnapped her. We really don't have much to go on."

Mia cocked her head at Malachi. It seemed to pain him to

agree with Thomas, but he did. "If there's nothing inside," he told her, "he's right."

"But there's a door. She could be right under our feet!"

"They wouldn't leave her unguarded," Malachi argued. "And they wouldn't lock this from the outside, unless..."

When he stared down at the door handle, she demanded, "Unless what?"

Cahill didn't want to answer, and Thomas was used to being the bearer of bad news, so he did it for him. "Unless they left her to die."

Mia staggered. Cahill grabbed her arm. "You stay here with Mann," he told her. "I'll check what's down there."

Thomas shoved past them. "You both stay here. I'll go."

Neither protested. Thomas lifted the door, hinges squeaking from decades of sun and sand. Steps led down into darkness. He took out his Glock and picked up the flashlight Cahill had left on the ground. Flicking it on, he saw cobwebs, dust, a fleeing roach. The dust on the steps looked mottled, as though someone had recently disturbed it, but it was too messed up to get a decent tread print.

"You need backup." Cahill took out his own weapon. "We have no idea what you're walking into. I don't need your death on my conscience."

Thomas gave him a grin. "Seems like a minute ago you were ready to kill me."

"I still might when this is over."

Thomas waved him off. "You're a Boy Scout, Cahill. You're better at protect-and-serve than assassination."

"Stay here," Cahill said to Mia. He handed her the crowbar. "We'll be right back."

Her features filled with indignation. "I'm not waiting while you two go down there." She lifted her chin, glaring defiantly. "Whatever is there, I can handle it."

"It may be dangerous," he argued.

She stepped around his big body, pocketing the earring and nodding at Thomas, "Let's go."

Yep, Thomas liked her a lot.

"Mia—" Cahill started.

She whirled on him. "Don't *Mia* me." Her voice shook and her breathing came in tight gulps. Thomas figured she probably needed her dog. Ronni had guessed Mia had PTSD after her ordeal and used the animal as a coping mechanism. "Please, Malachi. I have to...do this."

Cahill hesitated, but caved after a few seconds. He grabbed her and tugged her behind him. "Remember my conditions?"

She resisted slightly, then gave in and stayed put. "Yes."

Thomas hid his grin. These two were something else. "Both of you follow me, hands on shoulders. If I stop, you stop. When I go, you follow."

He felt Cahill's hand land on his left shoulder as he faced the steps. Cahill explained to Mia to mimic his action and put her hand on his. Then he gave Thomas a squeeze. "Ready."

"Go," Thomas said, and they went.

TWENTY

Mia covered her nose, the strange underground room filled with organic smells that turned her stomach and made her eyes burn. Who knew what had seeped into the ground besides ricin? The whole area was probably toxic, regardless of what the government claimed. A spider skittered down the wall on her left and she shivered. It would die soon or end up radioactive.

The room held empty shelves, rotting from the environment and neglect. A few had various machines and scales, boxes of gloves, and empty bins. A large red metal container had a hazardous sticker and they stayed a good distance from that.

"Ah." Thomas illuminated a tall chest against the far wall. "What's your guess, Cahill? What is someone hiding in that baby?"

Mia glanced around Malachi's shoulder to scrutinize the thing. It was black and dusty, with a gold outline and a center dial. A safe.

"Formulas? Drugs?" Malachi speculated.

Mia wondered why they would put it down here. "Seems like an odd place to store sensitive material."

"I'll have Coop send a locksmith." Thomas led them on. "There's another door up ahead."

Once more, Mia had to peer around Malachi's large frame. Thomas' light bounced off metals bars and another shiny lock on the handle. Thomas shone his beam as Malachi took the crowbar from her. "Looks like there's a tunnel beyond," Thomas told them.

He moved out of the way and the clang of metal on metal echoed loudly as Malachi stepped in. Mia covered her ears. He tossed the broken lock aside a moment later and handed the crowbar back to her. "We're going south."

He and Thomas exchanged a glance, then at the same time said, "Landfill."

"Why would the lab have an underground tunnel to that?" She shivered as realization hit, Sam's words coming back to her. "Oh, for the...disposal stuff."

Malachi appeared grim, the shadows adding to his demeanor. "Easier and less obvious to prying eyes if you can transport it underground."

They reformed their snake chain and headed in. The scent intensified and Mia thought, *this is what death smells like.*

Then it hit her—the chemical odors that had been burned into her nostrils during her captivity. "Funeral home."

They kept walking, but Malachi glanced at her. "What?"

"Embalming fluid—the smell I couldn't figure out before—they use it at funeral homes, right?" She stopped and her hand fell from his shoulder. "I remember it at my grandmother's service when I was eight." It was the only funeral she'd ever been to. "Could that be the chemical?"

Malachi reached back and squeezed her hand. "For sure

and that's helpful. Let's finish checking this out, then we'll notify the others."

He returned her hand to his body, and they started forward again. Her mind whirled. They'd held her hostage at a funeral home? Seemed unlikely, but it felt as though a dam had broken. She remembered the cloying scent of old carnations. Them and gladiolus flowers.

Funeral flowers, her mother had referred to them once, as they'd passed buckets of them at the grocery store not long after Grandma Ann had died. Tears had sprang into her mother's eyes, "I prefer roses," she'd claimed. "Yellow ones. Happy flowers."

More flashbacks pushed into Mia's mind with each step deeper into the tunnel. Things she had forgotten, purposely hidden from herself, like seeing her beloved grandmother in that casket. She had appeared as though she were sleeping, and at any moment would open her eyes and draw Mia into a hug.

But she hadn't, and just as unnerving, Mia had seen her mother break down and sob for the first time in Mia's young life. Her mother had always been so strong, and she'd never cried in front of her children again, until Mili was diagnosed with leukemia.

"Mia?"

She'd let go of Malachi. He was looking at her funny.

"Sorry." She blew out a breath and refocused on him. "I'm starting to remember a lot of things."

He patted her arm. "That's good. I promise as soon as we're out of here, we'll talk about all of it."

They marched on. Thomas thoroughly investigated the tops and sides of the tunnel, but even he drew up his jacket collar, holding it against his nose. "At least, there's no—" A squeak sounded and something raced passed their feet making

Mia jump and cry out. "Rats," he finished. "God, I hate vermin."

The ground began to rise again, the hint of fresh air teasing their nostrils. It still stank, but of garbage now and less of chemicals. The exit steps were bare metal bars sunk into the ground. They climbed out, Mia's boots not slipping.

Thomas lifted a metal grate and they exited to find themselves in a large garage.

Parts in various stages of decay and rust sat abandoned. Three car bays and several work benches filled the center. Oil cans, sockets, and tires were scattered about, and there was a healthy assortment of posters of naked women, license plates, and a steering wheel clock on the wall. "A chop shop?" Malachi asked.

"Looks like it," Thomas pointed toward the clock. "A functioning one, too."

Mia glanced at it, realizing the time was accurate. "Sam said the Feds and NSA have seen activity around here."

"Hmm." Thomas walked toward a black tarp, covering a large vehicle. "The landfill is a great place to hide stolen cars and extra parts." He raised a corner, flipping a section back to show them what was under it. "Does this look familiar?"

Malachi hit a wall switch and light flooded the room. "I'll be damned," he said, eyeballing the SUV.

Mia's heart hammered. "This is one of theirs, isn't it?"

"What do you want to bet we'll find Amber's DNA inside?" Malachi asked.

Thomas drew out his phone. "Time to call this in."

TWENTY-ONE

The next hour flew by in a flurry of information, the ball of thread finally unwinding.

Inside the Taskforce office, Sam, Joe, Cooper, Thomas, Ronni, Caleb, Bobby, Malachi, and Mia gathered, helping themselves to pizza and sandwiches while they walked through every piece of the case.

Sam had a whiteboard set up with pictures of the suspects, notes, and locations. Malachi shared the fact Lopez was actually Horvat, and his theory regarding the Komosu.

Mia had talked all the way there, telling Malachi her memories and discussing the possibilities for Amber's whereabouts based on them. Joe had already ruled out a dozen or more funeral homes in the area that had no connection to Marcher or any of his shell corporations, but he dove in harder to find one that might, after learning of the chemical she'd smelled.

"Formaldehyde," Bobby said, typing at his laptop. "Used in building materials, household products, vaccines, cosmetics insulation, glues and adhesives. You name it."

Malachi thought of the lab. "Vaccines?"

He read from the screen. "It's an antiseptic and kills most viruses, bacteria, and warts."

"Could they have used it at the lab?"

"I'm sure they did."

Malachi sat back. "And maybe Marcher found an inventory of it, but what would he use it for?"

"Torture," Thomas said. "Death. It's a gas that's corrosive to breathe and can cause a range of nasty symptoms. Mixed with a solution of water and injected directly under the skin, it can cause organ failure."

Ronni eyed him. "I don't want to know how you know that, do I?"

He looked grim and shook his head.

Ronni shuffled papers. "Amber's executive assistant had a file of anonymous emails and threats they didn't take seriously. I went through them again and found this. Same IP address as the cub one." She read it to them. "'You took the thing I love the most. Paybacks are a bitch.'"

"What does that mean?" Mia asked.

"His daughter." Harris sent a document around. "I have a friend with a specialized software program. She fed all the data we have into it, and came out with a fact I believe is the piece of the puzzle we've been missing."

Mia's mouth dropped when she read the print off. Malachi whistled softly under his breath as she showed it to him.

"Constance," she muttered. "Are you sure?"

Harris nodded. "It all checks out, once we knew where to look. Damon's real identity is Damon Marchesi. In high school, he got a woman named Linda Higt pregnant. She moved to Colorado and had a girl she named Constance. A few years later, she married a man whose last name was Cronenworth. He adopted the girl. When she grew up, she applied for and was awarded a full scholarship to U of Cal-San Diego. Her biological father probably had something to do with that stroke of luck."

Caleb set down a partially eaten slice. "I've got permission for Malachi to have a video conference with her. Want me to contact the warden and line it up?"

Harris looked impressed. "We should definitely question her."

Caleb wiped his hands and stood to make the call in the hallway. Joe leaned over and murmured to Malachi, "King's lawyer suggested the sting operation to the Feds offering to lure Newt to town."

"And get himself free in the process." Malachi grit his teeth. "Bloody bastard."

"Constance probably doesn't know," Harris said to Mia, ignoring the two of them. "But sending her to prison was Marcher's trigger."

Malachi tossed the paper on the table. "He had a daughter. I *knew* it was personal."

Mia sat back, that look of determination surfacing. "I should be the one to talk to her."

"Mia," Malachi started.

She cut him off. "I know her—*knew* her. I'm no agent but I'll be less intimidating than any of you. She's more likely to open up to me."

"I agree," Sam said.

Harris frowned and gave Sam a look suggesting she keep out of it. "You've never done anything like this, have you?" he asked Mia. "We need specific questions answered."

"So write them out," she countered.

She needed to feel useful. Malachi took Joe's notebook and flipped to a clean page. "Good idea."

Caleb returned. "Warden said fifteen minutes."

Thomas held up his phone. "Just got a text from one of my snitches. Newt Marcher is coming to town, and Lopez—Horvat —is on the hunt for Mia. Newt's offering a reward for her."

"What?" Mia blanched.

Malachi reached over and squeezed her hand. "Remember, you're safe."

She nodded, but he saw her throat constrict as she swallowed hard.

"Horvat has sided with Newt against King," Malachi stated. "Big surprise."

"No loyalty among criminals," Thomas added.

Harris pointed at Ronni. "We need intel on all incoming flights, including private."

She sidled up next to Bobby and he began typing. "On it."

"You know..." Thomas sat forward. "If Horvat is after Mia, we could pull a fast one on them both."

"No," Malachi said.

"What do you mean?" Mia asked.

Thomas tucked his phone away. "Use you as bait to capture him, get him to rat out King and cough up Amber's whereabouts."

Malachi wanted to skin him. Harris looked unhappy about the idea as well. "She's not bait," Malachi stated.

Mia studied Thomas. "I'll do it."

"Forget it," Harris intervened. "You're not going undercover."

Mia gripped the table. "It's my sister. I'll do whatever it takes to find her."

Harris stared her down. "No."

"But—"

He held up a hand. "I can have you escorted out of here and put on lockdown if you want to push me."

She pressed her lips together and sat back. "I don't like threats."

"I don't like a lot of things, Ms. Livingston." He shot a glare at Malachi, implying he was one of them. "But your safety and that of my team is my first concern. I will not jeopardize either in order for you to like me."

Caleb finished his pizza. "Um, better get those questions ready. Clock's a-tickin'."

The team all pitched in as Malachi wrote them out. He secretly admired Mia's gumption with Harris. He and Thomas instructed Malachi on additional questions, and Sam prepped her on how to handle the interview. When the call came through, she was ready. The rest of them stayed out of the camera's view.

"Constance," Mia said. "Thank you for speaking with me tonight."

"Mia?" The woman on the other end appeared happily surprised. "They didn't tell me it was you who wanted to talk to me. It's good to see you. I'm so sorry about what happened."

Mia hesitated, then recovered. "I need to ask you about this man." She put the side-by-side pictures of Horvat up. Did you know him?"

"Leo. Yes."

Mia put the photo down. "How?"

A heavy sigh. "He was my boyfriend. He forced me to steal those funds."

Mia looked puzzled. "You never told us this. Why didn't you inform the police?"

"I couldn't! He threatened to kill my mother if I did."

Mia pretended to make a note. "That must have been frightening. Do you know where he is now?"

"No, and I hope he rots in hell."

Mia studied the list, held up another image. "Why did this man, Jamarion King, visit you? You do know who he is, right?"

Constance covered her eyes and nodded. Scrubbed her face. "He's a businessman, convicted of kidnapping you along with the other guy, his boss. He told me he worked for someone who was going to get me released."

"Did he say who?"

Her ponytail swung as she shook her head. "I thought he was blowing smoke."

"Where did Leo like to hang out?"

Her gaze trailed away as she thought about it. "He was big on changing his tattoos, his looks. He enjoyed dogs, I think. He was always going to pet shops, but he never talked about wanting a pet."

Malachi glanced at Caleb. His twin made a high-five motion in the air.

"Did you know he was in the Quattro Gang?" Mia asked.

"Not until after you were taken and I saw his picture—the one with the beard—on TV."

"Did he ever mention the Komosu or laundering money?"

"No. Was he involved in that, too?"

Mia didn't answer and went on. "Who did he hang out with? Do you remember any names?"

"Different men all the time. He did tell me he owed one a lot of money, and needed to find a way to get him off his back."

"And that's why he forced you to steal from the election campaign?"

A nod. "I wanted to help him."

Mia went down the list again. "Do you know the identity of your birth father?"

She appeared taken aback. "No, why? My mother never said anything about him. When I brought it up, she told me she wasn't sure who he was, that it was a one-night stand."

"We believe it was Damon Marcher, leader of the gang that Lopez belonged to."

The woman covered her eyes again. "Oh Mia," she said through her hands. "That can't be. Are you sure?"

"Yes. I'll send you the details the FBI has uncovered."

"I can't believe it. Why? Why would he hurt you?"

"Because Amber sent you to prison."

She looked heartsick, eyes lowering. "He knew I was his daughter and he never told me?"

Mia gave Constance a moment to process it, then steered her back to their current situation. "We believe Leo has Amber. That's why I need you to tell me everything you can about him."

She appeared horrified and began to cry. "You and your sister were so good to me. I got screwed up, thought I was in love with that asshole."

Mia nodded as though she understood. "We need to catch him, Connie. His real name is Josip Horvat. Anything you can tell me could help."

"He even lied about his name?" She reclined, wiping tears from her cheeks. "This is a lot to take in."

"I'm aware, and you're doing great. What else can you tell me regarding him? Any idea where he might be holding Amber?"

"I don't know. I can't think straight right now."

Mia glanced at Malachi. He made a slicing motion with his finger, letting her know to end it. "Okay, if you do remember anything more, have the warden call the FBI so you can tell them. It's very important."

"I really am sorry. If there's anything I can do to make it up to you and Amber, I'll do it."

Mia's face pinched, and Malachi could tell she felt sorry for the woman. "I appreciate that. I'll put in a good word for you with the parole board when it's time."

After the call, Mia stood and shook out her arms. Malachi rubbed her back and the others resumed their seats, all talking at once.

Malachi motioned to Caleb. "Tell them about the Komosu and the pet shop."

His twin rattled off the details and theory they'd discussed. Harris assigned Sam to get as many law enforcement officers investigating those places as possible.

"I want to enact Thomas's plan," Mia said abruptly.

Malachi gripped her arm. "No way."

Harris agreed. "Not an option." He glared at Mia when she protested and she made a frustrated noise in the back of her throat, but gave up. He glanced at Malachi. "Take her home. I'll call once we have any leads."

TWENTY-TWO

Mia refused to speak to Malachi on the drive to her apartment. He didn't like being in the cold zone and her freezing him out, but she held firm, the cloudy night as dark as her mood.

Was this their first fight?

Once they were in the door, Ladybug and Taz were happy to see her. She greeted both animals in return with kisses. She'd missed Ladybug's pill time, so she gave each of them an extra helping of food, tucking the medicine into the dog's favorite treat to disguise it. Ladybug woofed up the snack with gusto, and then spit out the pill.

"Ladybug," Mia scolded. "You have to take your medicine."

Malachi went to the fridge and found a loaf of bread, laughing under his breath. She wanted to kick him, but stood back as he retrieved the pill and wrapped a partial slice around it. He bent and offered it to Ladybug coaxing her to take it. Mia was even more aggravated when her dog gobbled it down.

"Traitor," she muttered, then rounded on Malachi. "We're well past the ideal window to find a missing person. Dozens of leads, but not one points directly at a location for Amber. Please let me talk to Thomas and—"

He grabbed her up and kissed her.

She resisted, pressing her hands against his chest, but with no real force. It felt good to be in his arms, to feel his lips on hers. Even though she tried to continue arguing in between him taking her lips and then her neck, she finally began the descent into the bliss he always brought. "You play...dirty," she murmured against his mouth.

"I play to win," he countered.

He continued to kiss her into submission, as he moved them into her room. As he was undoing her bra, he said, "If you're too pissed for this, just say so."

He was so deadpan, she wasn't sure if he was being sarcastic or serious. She smacked his arm. "Take your pants off and get into bed."

For the next hour, he made her a very happy woman, and eventually they fell asleep, her spooning into him.

When she woke, it was daybreak, and the smell of coffee teased her nose. She was satisfyingly achy all over from his lovemaking.

She took a moment to simply stretch and listen to the homey sounds of him in her space, talking to Ladybug and rustling in the cupboards. Slowly, she rose, going to the bathroom to relieve herself and splash water on her face. When she came out, she found him at the kitchen table with Ladybug at his feet.

Every inch of the tabletop was covered. A map of the city, lists that Sam and Bobby had provided last night, his cell, and several colored pens. He was marking things on the map and talking to Caleb on speakerphone.

Tying her robe's sash, she leaned down and greeted him

with a kiss. He smiled warmly at her. She got a cup of coffee and sat across from him, eyeing the papers.

"Thanks, bro," he said to Caleb. "We'll be at the office soon. Have Josie call those media outlets for me." He disconnected.

"Media outlets?" Mia raised a questioning brow.

"A plan of mine."

Ladybug wanted up in her lap, so she lifted her and motioned at the map. "What's all this?"

He rubbed a hand across his eyes, taking a sip. "I'm tired of hoping the Feds find Amber. Time for me to do what I do best."

She gave him a cheeky grin. "Make love to me?"

His return smile was devilish. "Don't tempt me. I meant bounty hunting."

"Looks fun, can I come?"

She expected him to say no, and he didn't disappoint. "It's too—"

"Dangerous, I know. I'm getting tired of that excuse. Can't you tell? I love danger." Technically she loved him... but how could that be? She wasn't sure, it was too fast. Yet, she could feel it in her heart, her gut, through her whole body. Could it simply be the aftereffects of his lovemaking again? She barely knew him, but there it was. Amber would say it was infatuation, but this was different than anything Mia had felt before. "By the way, I've proven I can handle it."

He frowned, but there wasn't much consternation in it. "For now, I'm keeping you close for safety reasons, not because you can handle it. The situation could change rapidly, and seriously get too risky for you. I won't take that chance. You're too important to me."

She kissed Ladybug's head, set her down, and went over to slide into his lap. He scooted the chair back to make room for her and she faced him, teasing her fingers through his hair.

"You're important to me, too. If you're going into a life-threatening situation, then I'm going with you. You can bristle and yell all you want, but you're stuck with me. You better get used to it."

He gave her a patient smile and patted her butt. "Okay, here's the deal. Like before, you have to do what I say, when I say, and how I say it. Agreed?"

In answer, she kissed him, long and deep. "I promise."

He looked slightly dazed from the kiss, and she climbed off his lap, a satisfied grin on her lips. "We're gonna need some fuel. Let me go see what I can find to make for breakfast."

There was one egg and two slices of bread left. She pulled out a skillet, added a few frozen mushrooms, along with a slice of ham, and went to work.

"We've been going about this all wrong," Malachi pocketed his phone, pointing to some of the circles on the map. "This is the lab and the landfill. Over here is the place where Marcher was caught with you in his trunk. The other two sites the FBI raided are way across town. I'm eliminating them from our search. Even though they meet some of the criteria, I don't think Marcher and his crew were using those."

She glanced over. "What are those other three circles?"

"Known Komosu hangouts."

"So there's been no word from Sam or the others that they've tracked down Horvat?"

"None, but Newt Marcher landed in L.A. two hours ago. Dupé didn't have him arrested in hopes he might lead us to Horvat, King, or possibly Amber."

Her hands trembled slightly. She cracked the egg into the skillet and it sizzled. "So what are you and I going to do, Mr. Bounty Hunter?"

"We're hitting the streets," he told her with a gleam in his eye. "It's time we apprehend a fugitive."

TWO HOURS LATER, they were in front of Bondsmen Brothers with a full cast of news media waiting for them. Malachi, dressed in full fugitive apprehension gear, held up the photo of Horvat and cameras snapped. His voice boomed over the sidewalk and street, the microphone shoved toward him, unnecessary. "We're looking for this man, wanted for questioning in the kidnapping of Mayor Livingston, and we're asking for the public's help. There is a reward."

Inside the building, Caleb, Joe, Josie and Mia watched. Caleb chuckled. "I can't believe he's doing this."

Mia smiled, proud. "He's smart and quite brave."

"Absolutely," Joe agreed, "especially since he hates the spotlight. He'll never be able to hide under his comfortable rock again."

"He's been different ever since he met you," Josie told Mia.

Caleb drummed his fingers on a chair near the wall. "I'm honestly surprised he didn't try this last year when he was after Horvat. Maybe the guy wouldn't have duped him. Still, it *is* hard to believe he's going out on a limb like this, putting us on national TV. The Bureau will be so pissed."

Joe's phone rang at that exact moment. "Uh, huh," he said. "And there it is, my favorite federal agent calling. I'd say you're correct. Should I answer it?"

"Of course." Josie shot him a duh look. "She's also your wife."

Caleb winked at him. "Wouldn't want to be you right now, bro."

"Wait a minute." Mia glanced at the others. "What did you mean about Horvat duping Malachi last year?"

"Gotta take this." Joe hustled off. Sam's voice rang out before he ducked into his office and shut the door.

Caleb shook his head. "Um, nothing. I mean... He didn't tell you?"

Mia pinned them with a glare. "No. How about you do the honors."

It wasn't a question. Caleb looked out the window, avoiding her gaze. "Malachi feels guilty because he didn't collar Horvat before your kidnapping. He's been a bear about it since the beginning. Horvat was actually a skip trace for us; he's been on our books for nearly two years. We never carry any that long, especially not one that my twin is after. Malachi's the best at tracking these assholes, but we're all better than that. It just seemed like he was the one that got away. Every lead was a dead end. When you were kidnapped and we found out Lopez—Horvat—was behind it, he went crazy."

Weird emotions hit her. Realization did, too. She thought back to that day in the library, that night at the peer group meeting. Was it coincidence that Malachi had shown up at both? Was he helping her simply out of a sense of guilt?

She took a step back. "I see," she said, even though she didn't. "That must be what he meant about owing me."

Josie seemed to understand the conflict going on in her heart. She grabbed Mia's arm, giving it a squeeze. "We can all see he's totally infatuated with you. No one here wants to find Amber more than he does, but it's not only because Horvat outsmarted him—he's head over heels for you."

For a brief second, Mia considered calling Sue for a ride. She needed to think. Clear her mind. Sort this out.

But where would she go? Her apartment would never be the same, Malachi's presence would always be there. Her parents'? She wouldn't be alone or able to think there, although getting a hug from her mom would sure be nice. Seeing her dad, too.

Malachi stormed through the entrance, looking like he'd just been through hell. "Where's Joe?"

"Here." Joe rushed out, pocketing his phone. "Does anyone know a good divorce lawyer? I'm pretty sure Sam is going to kick me out."

Malachi touched Mia's arm. "You okay?"

This is about Amber, not me. "I'm fine."

Malachi nodded, looking at each of them in turn. "We're playing possum here. The Taskforce and Dupé will be on our asses any minute."

"They already are," Joe said. "Sorry to throw you under the bus, Mal, but I pretended I had no idea you were going to do that."

"You're off my Christmas list," he retorted with all seriousness. "But that's exactly what you needed to do. Pretend I've gone rogue, okay? If you end up having to talk to any of them, play dumb. This is all me. Meanwhile, Caleb and Joe, you hit the list of places I gave you. Josie, you coordinate things from here and man the phones. Someone, somewhere, has seen this bastard and they will call for that reward, I guarantee. Rats are rats. If there's money involved, one of his friends will turn on him."

Caleb and Joe began suiting up, filling their vest pockets with various items. Josie nodded. "You did good, Malachi. I like this plan." She glanced at Mia and gave her a wink.

"Mia and I are going back to the lab and landfill after I ruffle some feathers," Malachi told them.

Mia would confront him later regarding Horvat and what happened. About him owing her. "We've already searched those locations."

"That's where you were held," he said. "I'm sure of it, and we didn't go inside the lab itself. The SWAT team was looking for Amber, they might have missed something that will ring a bell with you. Now that we know about the false floor and tunnel, I want to check for more hidden spots. See if we find other clues. Horvat and King will believe the place is safe, now that it's been searched. If Horvat decides he needs to go into hiding, that may be where he returns."

Mia was skeptical. "They might come back?"

His eyes were hard, zealous. "It's a possibility, and if so, I want to beat them there and get my own eyes on it. I'm going to put cameras up, inside and out. Horvat will be wanting to hide since I've just made him too hot for King and Newt. He'll need to lay low. What better place than an abandoned building the Feds have already crossed off their list? We're going to hit a couple of different spots, too—pet shops, Komosu territory, you name it. We're going to talk to street people near those venues and flash Horvat's picture everywhere. We will find him, Mia, and in turn, your sister."

"At least we'll be doing something rather than sitting around analyzing stuff."

"If we catch him," Malachi told her, "we have a way better chance of getting him to turn on King and cough up Amber's location. If Newt's here, Amber's running out of time."

Caleb systematically checked his pockets once more. "Don't do anything stupid, Mal. If you sight Horvat or get a lead, wait and we'll get there ASAP to help with the takedown. He's a slippery SOB, and he's also incredibly savage."

The three brothers exchanged hand clasps and back pats, then Malachi grabbed Mia by the arm and began suiting her up.

TWENTY-THREE

Three hours later, Malachi had nothing and he was damn frustrated. After showing Horvat's photo to dozens of people, he was still empty handed.

What he did have was a tail. Not a Taskforce member, like he'd expected after ignoring multiple calls and messages from Harris. No, this was an older Subaru, exactly like the ride service woman—Sue—drove.

Mia was crossing another place off their list when he pulled over, waiting for the Subaru to do the same. As anticipated, it stayed several cars back, parking behind a delivery van.

Malachi checked the rearview, thinking on his options. "Stay here. I'll be back in a minute."

"Where are you—"

He shut the door on her question and purposefully strode to the sidewalk, keeping out of the sight of the Subaru and using the van for cover.

With his back pressed against the vehicle, he crept forward, until he could see the front bumper of the car. He leaned forward enough to confirm the ride sticker in the windshield's upper corner. What the hell? Who was this woman? FBI? One of King's crew?

The insider in the mayor's office?

Pushing off the side panel, he rounded the rear and glared at her. Sue startled, and then frantically searched for something on the passenger seat.

He strode to her window, knocked on it. She whipped around with a stun gun in hand, and pointed at him. She yelled for him to back off.

"Get out of the car," he ordered.

She stared, eyes wide, the stun gun still aimed at him.

"You realize it won't do anything but hit the glass, right?"

She looked embarrassed as she rolled the window down, still pointing it at him.

With one quick movement, he disarmed her, making her cry out from the unexpected action. "Hey, that's mine. Give it to me."

He twirled it around in his hand, walked back to the sidewalk, and motioned with his finger for her to follow.

With a great show of exasperation, she got out, closing the door quickly when another vehicle drove by and then reluctantly joined him.

He held out the weapon and she took it. "Why are you following me?"

"I'm not at liberty to say."

Mia burst from Malachi's truck and came running back to them. "Sue? What are you doing here?"

"You okay?" she asked.

Mia looked confused. "Fine. What's going on?"

"I didn't trust this guy." She waved a thumb in Malachi's direction. "I wanted to make sure he is on the up and up."

Mia studied Malachi, as if she were inspecting him for the first time. "I haven't quite decided that myself."

The two women ogled him, as if they could tell if he were a good guy or a bad one simply by his looks. He raised his hands palm up to Mia. "What are you talking about?"

Mia gave him a cute smile. "He's okay, Sue. You don't have to worry about me. He's a good guy."

Malachi shook his head. *Women.* He wasn't sure he'd ever understand them.

Sue touched Mia's arm. "I know who you are. I've known all along, but don't hate me, please? Your sister hired me to watch out for you and befriend you after you...you know."

"Amber hired you?" Her tone was incredulous. "But she didn't even know my—"

Sue waved it off. "I want you to know, I really do think of you as a friend. That's why I was worried after her kidnapping. I didn't know what to do when he was at your place yesterday. I was trying to keep an eye on you, because I was worried. I want to help locate Amber."

"We've got everybody searching for her. I don't know what you can do, but I feel the same way about you. I'm glad we're friends, although I'm a little pissed at her for doing this and not telling me."

"She's definitely a big sister," Sue said with a chuckle. "She has the gene and wants to look out for you. She told me that she felt guilty for your kidnapping. She said, 'I lost one sister already.' and that she was going to spend the rest of her life trying to make it up to you."

Malachi held out Horvat's picture. "Have you ever seen this man?"

Sue studied it briefly. "I wish I had. I'd go shoot him myself. I saw you on the TV, flashing the photos, but up to that point? I don't think I've ever seen him."

Mia hugged Sue. "Go on home. I'll contact you as soon as I

know something, and I'll check in with you tomorrow, even if I don't. Deal?"

"I'm just a text or call away."

They hugged again. Mia and Malachi returned to the pickup. He banged his hands against the steering wheel, frustrated.

Mia touched his arm. "What's next?"

Malachi started the engine. "The lab."

He drove right up to it this time, not hiding but staying wary all the same. There were no other vehicles, and the place looked as dead as ever. Gathering a bag of cameras from the back, he climbed out, hand on his weapon, just in case. He made Mia stay inside, while he made sure they were alone. Once he was, he motioned for her to join him at the rear entrance.

As she climbed the stairs next to the ramp, she stopped and looked at the dilapidated delivery truck next to the dock.

"What is it?" Malachi asked. "Another memory?"

She whirled, started back down the steps, snapping her fingers. "This." The white panels were dingy and dirty. She smacked the side of one with a gloved hand. "There's something about it that's bugging me."

He felt the rush that he always got when something clicked into place. He moved to the rear double doors. There was another padlock. It didn't look as pristine as the one on the basement tunnel, but it still didn't seem as old as he expected from the condition of the truck. Had someone purposefully made it appear more broken-down than it was? "They transported you in this?"

"Maybe," she said, looking sick.

Even if her mind didn't know it, her body did. He'd seen similar reactions from others like this.

He made quick work of breaking the lock. He and Mia

stood shoulder to shoulder, as they opened the doors. The inside was shadowed and he flicked on his flashlight, shining it around the interior. "Well, I'll be damned."

She flinched. "That's...it."

A walk-in refrigeration unit, complete with a drain at the center of the floor.

"Cahill?" It was Thomas, once again coming out of nowhere and making them both jump. "Boy, you get around."

Mia sank down on the edge of the loading dock, hand going to her heart, her breath coming in gasps.

Thomas strode up the ramp. "What did you find?"

Malachi bent down beside her. "Look at me. You're okay. You're in control. Just breathe." To him, he said, "We found where they held Mia."

Thomas eyed the vehicle and nodded. "Interesting. They could move her at a moment's notice."

Mia burst out in tears and reached for Malachi. He took her by the arms, turning her to face him. "I'm right here, and we're a step closer now to finding Amber."

Thomas stalled, a look of fear on his face. A woman crying could do that to the toughest man around. "He's right. This is good news."

Lips quivering, her tearful gaze rose to Malachi's. She searched his face. "I know about...Horvat. How you failed to capture him. Are you only helping me to relieve your guilt?"

Malachi felt like he'd been punched in the gut. The pain in her eyes stole his breath. "Of course not. I would help you regardless of how I felt, but I'm all in. I seriously was not stalking you that day in the library. It was a coincidence. I didn't even recognize you at first. Like Sue, what happened between us is..."

She was gasping for air again, and he drew her to her feet, encircling her in his arms. "Shh. It's okay. I know the memories are awful, but you're not them. You're a strong, confident, intelligent woman. You have the strength to overcome this. I'm right here with you, and I'll do anything to help. I'm totally—"

Thomas's phone rang. "Sorry. It's Coop. I gotta take this."

Mia's breathing became easier. She wrapped her arms around Malachi's waist. "You're what?" she whispered.

"Head over heels infatuated? Stone cold in love with you? Take your pick."

He heard Thomas speaking off in the background, but he kept his focus on Mia. The bastards who had done this to her were going to pay. He was going to make sure of it.

"There's no way..." she sucked in a breath. "You can't be."

He chuckled, feeling her relax and her breathing becoming more normal. "I usually do things by the book, but in case you haven't noticed, you've blown that book all to hell. I don't want to scare you, and I don't want to come on too strong, but I'm not kidding about my feelings."

She took a long, deep breath, and laughed. "You better reconsider. My life has been a horrid disaster for the last year and a half, and I'm a hot mess because of it."

He set her back gently, keeping his arms on her shoulders, as he gazed into those eyes he'd come to love. "I usually run like hell from messes, but do you see me going anywhere?"

She smiled through her tears. "I'm glad you're here. Honestly, I'd be lost if you weren't."

Malachi wiped the tears from her face, and as Thomas rejoined them, he picked up a bag. "We're going to need this vehicle analyzed."

"Already on it." Thomas told them. He glanced at Mia. "You good, Livingston?"

Her gaze went down rather than to the open doors of the van. "I can smell it, can you? Rotten flowers. Embalming fluid."

She was right. Malachi detected it now, too. "At some

point, they disguised it as a florist van, and who knows what they were actually transporting in it. Drugs, guns, people." It had a high ceiling, nine-foot at least, and it would be easy, even for him, to stand upright in it. All this time they'd been looking for a building.

Mia took a deep, audible breath and met both his and Thomas's eyes. "I'm good."

"What's in the bag?" Thomas asked.

"Cameras, in case Horvat or King come back." Malachi tossed it at him. "Make yourself useful."

TWENTY-FOUR

I nside, they went to work.

Malachi kept one eye on Mia as they did. She was shaky, but determined, and she and Thomas helped him connect the cameras through a Wi-Fi system that he installed in a cabinet to hide it.

They checked for additional false floors or fake walls, searching for any kind of room that might hold Amber, but came up with nothing. Dusty and tired, they called it quits, and Malachi picked a cobweb from Mia's hair as they exited the building and jogged down the steps of the dock.

"Well, well, who do we have here?" The man's voice brought all three of them up short.

"Horvat." Malachi's stomach twisted. A limo was hidden in the shadow of the delivery truck. The asshole had two men with him holding guns, and another dressed in a tasteful, expensive suit. He looked like a younger, thinner version of his father. "And Newt Marcher."

"Very good," Marcher said. "I don't believe we've met."

"Hands up," a man with a semi-automatic demanded in

heavily accented English. He and his gun-wielding companion appeared to be Asian. Nervous ones, at that. Their hands both shook, making the weapons tremble.

Thomas and Malachi did as instructed. Mia didn't. She stepped toward Horvat. "Where's Amber? Where is my sister?"

"Don't!" Malachi reached for her, but he was too late.

Horvat grabbed her and jerked her to him, wrapping his arm around her neck and producing a pistol. H smiled and pointed it at her temple. "It's been a while, my lovely Mia." He rubbed the side of his cheek against hers and she whimpered, eyes suddenly wild. "Be a good girl and don't move, or I'll blow your brains out."

Newt laid a hand on him. "Not yet." He glanced at Thomas and Malachi. "All I want is for my sister to be released from jail. I get her, you get both Livingstons."

He sounded like a suave businessman making a casual deal. It rankled Malachi's nerves. "Hurt her and you'll die."

Horvat snorted. "I get this one, regardless. That was our deal."

Mia made a mewing sound in the back of her throat, her eyes locked on Malachi. He tried his best to show her he wasn't scared.

It was a lie.

Newt regarded Horvat with a cool gaze. "Do I need to remind you of your screwup? That you failed to take care of Mr. King, as you promised? When you don't hold up your end of a deal, I don't hold up mine."

"I'll make a call." Thomas pointed at his pocket. "My boss will cut a deal for the mayor."

"Why do you want Constance?" Mia asked through gritted teeth.

"She has something of mine." The slick smile returned, with a touch of greed thrown in. "I need it back."

Like what, Malachi wondered. Didn't matter—he had to make a compromise here and save Mia. "Constance means nothing to the Feds. They'll be happy to make the exchange, but only if Mia walks away unharmed."

Newt shrugged and examined his nails. "Constance was the one thing my father loved in this world. He didn't even know her and yet..." Anger flashed across his face. "He betrayed me. Betrayed all of us over her."

"So you want to kill her? Because your father didn't love you?" Mia's hands gripped Horvat's muscled arm still around her throat. "She's already in jail, suffering, because this asshole made her embezzle from my sister."

Newt chuckled, but it was dry and without humor. "He and King should have kept their paws off her. Made Daddy very mad." He sounded like a psychopath, and Malachi fought his urge to jump him. "But I need her for another purpose."

"Like what?" Mia asked.

Newt grabbed her chin and Malachi stepped forward automatically. He got the barrel of a semi-automatic in his face, forcing him to pull up short.

"Our father gave her everything," Newt growled, "and she doesn't even know it."

Malachi suddenly understood—Constance had some kind of key to the Marcher assets. Had to be. Newt needed her to access them, but why would Marcher have left valuables with a daughter he hadn't even claimed?

"We'll get her released," Mal assured him. Keeping his gazed pinned on the psycho, he was sizing up Horvat, too. He could take him if Thomas could handle the other men, but that would leave Newt. How dangerous was he in his fancy suit? "Just let Mia go. She's worth nothing to you."

Thomas added, "The cops are on the way. Best to let us secure the exchange with my boss before they arrive. They get trigger happy in hostage situations. I guarantee if anything happens to the mayor's sister, there will be no deal."

Newt actually seemed to think this over.

Horvat goaded him. "Come on, already. Take their stupid offer or let me have the girl. Money or pleasure— I get one or the other or I'll kill you right here." He turned his pistol on Newt.

Mr. Slick cocked a brow, but otherwise looked unconcerned. "This is why you'll never rise above being the muscle, Josip. Your brain is the size of a pea."

Horvat's gun leveled between Newt's eyes. "And you've got no balls, you little dick. Your old man went soft on us, and he screwed us all over, liquidating his assets and putting them in that offshore account for your half-sister. Get real. That's the only reason I went after her, the only reason King got involved. We found out what he did. I should have killed him when I had the chance, and made Constance pony up, but here we are. *I want my fucking money.*"

Newt rolled his eyes and turned to Malachi and Thomas. "Do you see what I'm dealing with?" He appeared completely untroubled about Horvat going off script. "So hard to get loyal help these days." He glanced up at the sky, then back to Thomas. "Make the deal," he told him. "We'll be in touch." He motioned at Horvat. "Bring the girl. Let's go."

"Wait!" Malachi stepped forward, but the barrel of the gun was in his face.

Horvat dragged Mia to the limo, her cries echoing off the delivery truck's panel. She fought, heels dragging in the sand as she pounded at him with her fists.

"Stop it, bitch." He knocked her in the head with the butt of the gun.

Malachi saw red. With quick reflexes, he knocked the weapon in his face away. Mia went limp and a fresh wave of hot anger ripped through him as he ripped the gun from the henchmen's hand. The Korean had been ready to shoot, and it went off, the bullets peppering nearby trees.

A swift jerk and he nailed the guy in the stomach with the butt. Thomas jumped on the other henchman and more shots rang out.

Malachi's opponent squared his legs, hands raised, martial-arts style, and then came at him before he could fire. He kicked out and Malachi dodged, whipping around to avoid the blow, but the bastard kept coming. He knocked the weapon from Malachi's hands, and that pissed him off even more. He reared back and sent an uppercut into the man's chin. The Korean dropped and sprawled in the dust.

In the distance, sirens rode the wind. Mia's scream cut through the fight— she was conscious, but he caught sight of her being thrown into the limo. Malachi hopped over the downed man, raising the gun to fire at the tires.

The asshole kicked him in the back of the knee, and Malachi faltered, bringing the gun around to shoot the guy. An unexpected fist clocked him in the jaw. The weapon fell to the ground and they both scrambled for it.

Malachi knocked it away, hit the Korean again, and sent him to the ground. This time, he didn't get up.

Newt was closing the passenger door, but movement on his side caught Malachi's attention. Thomas was down, his attacker ready to shoot him in the face.

Any second, the limo would peel out, carrying Mia from him, but if Malachi didn't save Thomas, the guy was about to get his brains blown out.

Calculated risk. *Who do I save?*

Malachi drew his Glock and shot the henchman before he could kill Thomas. Then he pivoted and took off running as the vehicle took off.

The driver gunned it, and the back tires spun, kicking up sand and blinding him. He couldn't let them go, but he couldn't fire blindly, either. He might hit Mia.

The vehicle straightened out and the driver hammered the gas, sending the limo jetting down the road. Malachi ran all out, nearly catching it before it raced off and left him in the dust.

She's gone. He kept going, unwilling to give up. Far behind, he heard Thomas yell his name, but he wouldn't stop. He couldn't. Not his legs, not his heart.

What have I done? He wanted to die. He'd let Horvat get Mia again.

The sirens drew closer, a tiny flicker of hope lighted in his heart. Dodging off into the scrub brush and trees, adrenaline fueled him. He pumped harder, flying across the landscape, his memory from the previous night laying out a map for him. He would cut them off.

But he had to run faster.

Branches slapped his face, cacti jabbed his legs through his pants. He jumped over one of the fallen trees, scaring another snake.

Faster, goddammit. Don't let her down.

He burst through the brush near the abandoned building off the main road. Heart thumping so hard, he thought it might explode, he jetted past it and onto the road.

And got hit.

At his unexpected appearance, the driver had jerked the wheel. The limo swerved, the back end fishtailing. He jumped up but didn't clear the rear end, the bumper clipping him as it swung by.

He sailed through the air, trees and sky a blur. When he came down hard on his side, his body screamed in pain.

The limo went off the dirt road, the front end colliding with a tree. The crash echoed, his heart nearly stopping at the thought of Mia being thrown around inside. Dragging himself with his arms, his legs useless, he tried to get to her.

The passenger door flew open and she jumped out, face as white as a sheet as she ran toward him yards away on the other side. "Malachi!"

He heard tires behind him, the screech of breaks and sirens. Then his heart froze.

Horvat emerged, bleeding from his nose and a cut over his eye. He raised a gun and pointed at Mia's back.

Malachi had his weapon out in a flash. "Get down!"

Mia ducked. *Good girl.* At the same instant, a woman appeared next to him and a projectile flew through the air.

"Hey, asshole! You leave my friend alone!" Sue yelled.

The distraction caused Horvat to glance at the object flying toward him. Malachi squeezed the trigger.

The stun gun didn't even come close, but Horvat's head snapped back from the bullet.

Mia rose from her crouch and scrambled to Malachi. She hugged him, as Sue bent down to pat his shoulder. "You're starting to grow on me," she told him.

"Oh my god," Mia wheezed. "Are you okay?"

He assured her he was, even though the pain in his right leg was so bad, he was seeing stars.

Police rolled in, sirens blazing. The driver and Newt stumbled from the car, both falling to the ground. The driver was hurt bad; Newt not as much.

Mia rocked back and forth with him in her arms. "Malachi, what were you thinking? You could have been killed."

"I think my leg is busted." A fresh wave of fire shot through his groin and hip at her movements. "And I was saving you."

Thomas barreled up and grabbed Newt as the guy gained his feet.

Sue eyed Malachi's leg. "Nice shot."

He grinned through the pain. "You, too."

She held out a fist and he bumped it with his. "I need an ambulance," Mia screamed at the officers moving in to apprehend Newt. One seemed familiar—the detective from the other night.

"I want to cut a deal," the Marcher cub yelled over and over. "I know where the mayor is!"

Harris showed up at the same time the ambulance did. "You just couldn't let us handle this, could you, Cahill?"

"You had Mann dogging me every step of the way, and I let him." He grimaced as two techs lifted him onto a gurney. "You're lucky I didn't shoot him."

Thomas overheard the exchange, and gave Malachi a thumbs-up.

Harris chuckled. "You knew all along?"

"Of course I knew, but it was your case. I was being courteous." One of the EMTs instructed everyone to get out of the way, but Mia held onto Malachi's hand. Harris kept pace as he was wheeled toward the ambulance. "We'll expect payment for services rendered by closing today. If you have any questions, you can take them up with Josie."

Harris grinned. "You know the government doesn't move that fast cutting checks."

Thomas jogged up then and Malachi halted the EMTs from lifting him into the back. "Thanks, man," Mann said, and they exchanged a fist bump. "You saved my life."

"Anytime," Malachi told him.

"You need anything..." He thumped his own chest. "I'm here for you."

Malachi fought through the searing heat in his leg and the nausea starting in his gut. "Come to mention it, I do have a personality quiz I need you to fill out for my psych class."

Thomas looked amused. He wiped blood from his chin and

nodded reluctantly. "That wasn't quite what I was thinking, but okay, throw in a bottle of gin and I'm in."

"AMASS work?" At the man's nod, he told him, "You got it."

Mia attempted to climb in with him. The medic informed her she'd have to drive separately. She glared at the guy. "I'm going with him."

There was fire in her eyes, but Malachi grabbed her hand. "Go with Harris and the others. Get your sister. She needs you more than I do right now."

Mia climbed in anyway and kissed him. "Thank you," she whispered against his lips.

Then she jumped down and was gone.

TWENTY-FIVE

F*our days later*

MIA'S HEART had stopped when she'd seen Malachi go over the trunk of the limo and land on the ground. She'd had nightmares since then about the ordeal, but her therapist had assured her that was normal. Her subconscious was working through her fear that Malachi had ended up dead, even though he hadn't.

Thomas had convinced Cooper to allow her to go on the raid and retrieve her sister. The Komosu were holding her at one of their pet supply warehouses. Not only was she rescued, the FBI also confiscated billions of dollars in illegal weapons and the means the Komosu used for laundering the profits made from selling them. The safe held USBs and other incriminating evidence for the chop shop. A two-for-one, Ronnie had called it.

Hugging Amber had been the happiest day of her life.

Outside of a few bruises, she was okay. The two of them had rarely been separated since the moment Mia defied Director Dupé's orders to wait until the medics had checked Amber and declared her healthy before she rushed to her sister's side.

"Are you going to marry him?" Amber now asked as Mia carried Ladybug up the stairs to the second floor of the university library. The dog had a new vest, her papers tucked neatly inside the pocket.

Mia pinned the phone between her ear and shoulder. She shifted the dog, tucked under one arm, and attempted not to drop the books she'd shoved into her messenger bag, weighing down her other. "That's rushing it, don't you think? We haven't even had a proper date, yet."

Her sister laughed. "What you have goes way deeper than dating. I saw the way he looked at you when I met him at the hospital." She was back at work—life went on—but had confessed to Mia she was having trouble sleeping, and when she did, she had nightmares. "That boy is a goner. Life is short, MiMi. Better grab him while you can. He's a keeper, and you deserve a hero in your life."

The thought made her warm all over. "I gotta run. I'm at the library. Quiet space and all that."

"Nice try. Hang up on me and I'll cancel your ride home."

Mia sighed softly. "Are you threatening me?"

"Damn right, I am. Malachi passes all my tests with flying colors. In fact, I'm going to give him a key to the city as soon as his doctor releases him. It will be a big event—all the media outlets will be there, and I'll make sure he's properly thanked by the whole city. Maybe he'll pass Dad's yardstick then."

If anyone could placate their father, who believed no man was worthy of his daughters, it might be Malachi. "You ran a background check on him, didn't you?"

"What kind of sister would I be if I didn't look out for you?

I know everything about him, including the kind of socks he buys and his favorite brand of toilet paper. I had to make sure he's good enough for you, and wouldn't leave you high and dry."

Mia smiled. She hit the landing and took a left. "He's more than good enough."

"You're starstruck by those muscles."

She giggled. How long had it been since she'd done that? "They *are* pretty nice."

They shared a laugh. A loud sawing noise started up on Amber's end. "I'll see you tonight." She spoke over the grating sound. "I'm headed to a meeting with the city council. This may be a first—I'm actually looking forward to it."

"Constance is meeting us afterwards at South of the Border." Mia's mouth watered just thinking about the delicious food. It was so great to be out in the world again, not afraid of, well, anything. "I'm dying for a chimichanga."

"I can't wait. Love you."

"Love you, too."

Mia's pulse stuttered when she spotted a man sitting at her table. His right leg was in a cast, and a pair of crutches were propped against the wall. His expression reminded her of a thunderstorm, as he pecked away at his laptop.

The compound fracture had required surgery. Once the cast could be removed, he would need a lot of therapy. He'd been quite a bear over his injury, disappointed he wouldn't participate in the triathlon, but repeatedly insisting it was worth it to save her. She'd heard from Sam and Josie that he was making his brothers miserable, calling the office constantly, and trying to run the business from his hospital bed.

But he was the best thing she'd ever seen, all those muscles and that big brain of his combined together and sitting in her chair.

It was kind of cute that Ladybug and Malachi looked like twins with their bandaged limbs. She was just thankful that everyone was alive, and while he kept telling her he was in this for the long haul, she had to keep pinching herself. He was her dream.

She sauntered over, glaring down at him. "You're in my seat."

He glanced up, and the storm cloud broke, turning into a giant sunshine of a smile. "You're late."

Ladybug wagged her tail like crazy. "You're supposed to be in the hospital."

Malachi petted the dog under the chin. "I had to get out of there." He took the bag from her, placing it on the table. "They were driving me crazy."

She set the dog on the floor, and she went to her usual spot, climbing over Malachi's straight leg. "Did the doctor release you?"

His gaze went to his screen, avoiding hers. "Caleb snuck me out."

Of course he did. "And brought you here instead of taking you home? You should at least have your feet up."

"Mann finally filled out the personality quiz. To tell the truth, I'm scared after seeing the results. I can't tell if he's joking with these answers or if he's really as crazy as he makes himself sound. I only have a twenty-four hour extension to get this done and turned in with the rest of my report. Can you believe it? Professor Jones is a hardass."

She sat and removed the books from her bag. "Did you actually ask for a longer extension? After everything that's happened, I'm sure he would oblige."

He pretended to study the screen. "I needed to get out of that damn hospital and back to some semblance of normal. Joe and Caleb have been harassing me about being an invalid, and

I'm going to have to bribe Josie or Sam to fill out all that god-awful paperwork the Feds want done. This was the best excuse I could find to get away from all that."

She leaned forward and caught his eye. "Malachi, it's fine for you to take time and stay home, rest up. You could work there."

He peeked at her over the lid. "The view is better here."

She felt her cheeks heat. "Do you need help with your report?"

"If I say yes, will you come sit on my lap?"

She waggled a finger at him. "I'm not sitting on you, but I will help you if you truly need it. If I let you stay here, you do things my way, understood?"

He bowed his head, but she could see the smile teasing his lips. "Okay, okay, I agree to you turning the tables on me."

"Good." She liked ordering him around. She opened her laptop. "Wanna go to a meeting tonight?"

He studied her. "Do you need one?"

"We all do, and I'm bringing Amber."

"I'm in, if you want me to go."

"Why wouldn't I?"

He dropped his gaze again. Released a heavy sigh. "If I'd caught Horvat before he kidnapped you last year, none of this would have happened."

Ridiculous, silly man. "You're not the bad guy here, Malachi. Your blame is misplaced."

"That's why I was at the peer support group meeting that night. Harris had already told me the Bureau had cut a deal with King and that he'd immediately buddied up with Horvat the minute he was set free. I wanted to go after him, but was ordered to stand down. Anger and guilt were eating me alive, and I knew I needed a meeting. I hadn't been to one in months."

It seemed like luck or serendipity. She didn't care either way. "Maybe it was karma, putting you smack dab in the middle of what went down, so you could get justice and make amends at the same time. But enough is enough. I forgive you, even though there is nothing to forgive. End of story. Move on, okay?" She opened a book and studied the contents, looking for the chapter she needed. "How did you get here?"

"Sue drove me."

Traitor. "Funny, she didn't mention that when she dropped me off."

"I told her to keep it a secret."

Men. Mia chuckled, deciding she would have to have a long talk with Sue about her loyalties.

Malachi touched her hand. "I was actually hoping you'd demand I make more amends—like possibly for the rest of my life?"

She squeezed his fingers, heart racing at the look in his eyes. They'd survived so much together, still had a lot to go through with his therapy. They were *both* a hot mess at this point, but by god, they could do it together.

"I see." She tapped a finger to her chin, pretending to think it over. "I suppose if you do everything I tell you to, that could be arranged."

Even though he was in a cast, he boosted himself up and leaned across the table. She met him halfway and kissed him for all she was worth.

TWENTY-SIX

Mann brought the dog at 1500 hours. Malachi couldn't go to the foster's house to pick him up, but they'd done a video chat, and she had okayed the adoption. She'd even given him a discount, after realizing who he was, and using the term 'hero'. It made him flinch, but at least that was one good thing that had come out of his fifteen minutes of fame.

He'd instructed Caleb to send the dog rescue double the amount. Upon his arrival, the pit-mix seemed to realize that Malachi was his new buddy and jetted across the foyer into the living room, hopping up onto the couch and diving into Malachi's lap.

Malachi grunted, hugging the beast. The dog had to weigh fifty pounds or more, and the pressure on his bad leg hurt, but the enthusiasm Boomer displayed made him laugh through the pain.

"My work here is done," Mann said, turning for the door. "I'm still waiting for that gin, Cahill."

"Sue left a bottle of AMASS at the Bondsmen Brothers' office. You can pick it up there." Wrestling past the dog's face-licking, he glanced around. "Did you buy the stuff for him I asked for?"

"Yep. Got it in my car."

Mann returned a minute later with a plastic sack from the pet shop, Harris on his heels. The second man carried a giant bag of kibble and was wearing glasses.

"Goofing off again, I see," Harris goaded.

Boomer's nose lifted in the air and he jumped off Malachi's lap. "Do I want to know why you're here?" Malachi shot back.

Mann tossed the sack on the coffee table and started unloading its contents. Harris set down the dog food. "I hear you're gonna need this."

Didn't answer his question. "Thanks. What's with the specs?"

"Nothing." Harris whipped them off and tucked them in a jacket pocket.

"Celina's making him wear them." Mann flinched when Harris swatted him, then grinned as he pulled out a collar, bowls, toys, and a leash. "I also got extra in case you have guests. Another dog bowl and one for the cat."

His grin was cheeky. The dog immediately dove for one of the toys, claimed a spot on the floor, and began ripping it to shreds.

"What's the latest on Constance?" Malachi asked, as they watched the animal.

Harris was happier to discuss this subject. "She's been released from jail and is aiding us in finding the rest of Marcher's assets." He began picking up stuffing. Boomer tossed a wad in the air and started eating it.

Mann gently took hold of the dog's mouth and teased it out. Boomer, who had some sizable teeth, thought it was all in good fun, and kept trying to get it back.

"Ow," Mann yelped when Boomer bit him playfully. "I see we need to teach you some manners."

He hadn't broken the skin and there was no blood. "Don't be a baby," Malachi chided.

Boomer grabbed a second toy, a dolphin. This one appeared a bit tougher to destroy.

Harris shook his head at the dog. "Constance set up an offshore account for Damon, not knowing about his illegal enterprises at the time. He appeared to be a normal client, and she only ever spoke to him over the phone."

He journeyed into the kitchen, probably looking for a garbage can. Thomas continued. "Marcher had never written down the information, and Constance was the only one who had the details. She told her story to Dupé about Horvat forcing her to embezzle from Amber, and she still had the account numbers that she'd funneled those funds into, as well. What's left of the money will be returned to the mayor soon."

Harris returned and rolled his eyes as the dog ripped open the dolphin. Filling once more flew through the air and the dog's mouth. "Newt turned on King, and he's going to be in prison for a long time. No more deals. Baby Marcher is also in jail, and even though he coughed up the mayor and turned on the others, he won't see freedom anytime soon. How's Mia and her sister?"

"Mia's great." He couldn't keep the smile off his face. "Amber's okay. Mia said she's having nightmares. We're all attending a support group meeting tonight."

Mann grappled with Boomer for the wrecked toy. "I heard she's pushing for the Justice Department to throw everything they can at King and Newt."

"I hope they do."

Mann and Harris went back to removing the stuffing from the dog's mouth and throwing out the second toy. While they were doing that, the front door opened again, and Mia came in carrying Ladybug.

"You got him already?"

As she put a knee on the couch to lean down and kiss Malachi's forehead, Boomer rolled onto his back and showed his belly to Thomas. The man laughed and scratched it. "That's better, dog."

"It seems I'm kind of a hero around here," Malachi told her, letting a bit of pride flow into his voice. "The foster woman told me that Boomer is, too. He smelled smoke when a fire started in her house several nights ago and alerted her. She was able to put it out before it did too much damage, and she attributes that to him. She said we belonged together, and pushed the adoption right through."

Ladybug sniffed at the newcomer and wagged her tail hesitantly. Mia made an impressed face and set the terrier down. "How nice."

Malachi prayed the two dogs would get along, because it looked like they might be spending a lot of time together.

"By the way, since you *are* a local hero, Amber's planning an event to honor you."

"What?" His stomach clenched. "No, that's so not necessary."

Mia shrugged. "She's the mayor." She glanced at Harris and Mann. "She'd honor you and your team, as well, but doesn't want to blow your undercover stuff."

"Just doing our duty," Harris said. He and Mann backed away, heading for the front. Harris pointed at Malachi. "I hear you start therapy on Monday."

Malachi didn't like the glint in his eye. "Yeah...?"

"Don't think you're going to get out of it or have it easy. We've got to get you back in fighting shape. You might not be able to compete in January's triathlon, but I'm holding you to the next one. I'm doing it myself. We'll train together."

"What?" This day was going to hell in a hand basket. Malachi tried not to show any fear. "Appreciate the offer, but—"

"No buts." Harris winked at him and waved at Mia. "I'm going to put you through the wringer, Cahill. You'll love it."

Mann snickered as they went out. "I'll be by later to share the gin."

As the door closed, Boomer got up to check out the terrier and her bandaged leg. "That sounds like a fabulous idea," Mia said.

Malachi watched as the two dogs sniffed each other and Ladybug did a play bow, barking good-naturedly at the much bigger animal. She seemed to be letting Boomer know she was in charge. "When would having Cooper Harris attend your physical therapy session ever be a good idea?"

She laughed, holding out her hand to let Boomer sniff it before she petted him. "I meant about the triathlon. All of us should train for it, you, me, your brothers. Even Sam and Josie. Although, I better tell you—I'm not into exercise. I might be able to do the five-k walk. I'll mention it to Amber. It will be a good promotion for her. We can get T-shirts made and enter as a group."

Malachi groaned, smiling as well. His life was never going to be the same.

"Aw, you got bowls for Ladybug and Taz too?" She examined the dishes, one with a bone painted on it, the other with a cat figure. "That's so sweet."

Thank you, Mann. He reached out and grabbed her hand to tug her close. She sunk onto the couch and tucked her legs up under her, snuggling into him as he put an arm around her. Together, they watched Boomer grab the third and last toy, a knotted rope, and offer it to Ladybug. She accepted one end and they began a tug-of-war.

Boomer was gentle, as if understanding that Ladybug needed him to be, and for the first time in a long while, Malachi relaxed. Not only had he landed the love of his life, but he now had two dogs to make things even better. "All the chairs in my house?"

"What about them?"

He squeezed her shoulder. "They're all yours. Every one of them."

Mia pressed a hand to his chest where his heart was. "I love you, Malachi Cahill."

He placed his own over hers and brought her fingers to his lips. "I love you, Mia Livingston, and I'm never going to let you go."

As the dogs played, she turned his face so she could kiss him, keeping her gaze locked on his. As he stared into her beautiful green eyes, he knew he was lost. A goner. There would never be anyone else for him.

Joe and Caleb had found their happily-ever-afters, yet Malachi hadn't believed he ever would. Right here, right now, he knew that wasn't the case. Dreams did come true.

The future looked bright, and he couldn't wait to share it with the woman in his arms.

READY FOR MORE?

Don't want to miss a single release? Click here and get a FREE story (or two… :))

And if you enjoyed Malachi and Mia's story, join Misty's Official Fan Group to read an interview with them!

SEALs of Shadow Force Series

Fatal Truth

Fatal Honor

Fatal Courage

Fatal Love

Fatal Vision

Fatal Thrill

Risk

SEALS of Shadow Force Series: Spy Division

Man Hunt

Man Killer

Man Down

The SCVC Taskforce Series

Deadly Pursuit

Deadly Deception

Deadly Force

Deadly Intent

Deadly Affair, A SCVC Taskforce novella

Deadly Attraction

Deadly Secrets

Deadly Holiday, A SCVC Taskforce novella

Deadly Target

Deadly Rescue

Deadly Bounty

Deadly Betrayal

Deadly Threat

The Super Agent Series

Operation Sheba

Operation Paris

Operation Proof of Life

Operation Lost Princess

Operation Ambush

Operation Christmas Contraband

Operation Sleeping With the Enemy

The Justice Team Series (with Adrienne Giordano)

Stealing Justice

Cheating Justice

Holiday Justice

Exposing Justice

Undercover Justice

Protecting Justice

Missing Justice

Defending Justice

SCHOCK SISTERS MYSTERY SERIES w/Adrienne Giordano

1st Shock

2nd Strike

3rd Tango

The Secret Ingredient Culinary Mystery Series

The Secret Ingredient, A Culinary Romantic Mystery with Bonus Recipes

The Secret Life of Cranberry Sauce, A Secret Ingredient Holiday Novella

Paranormal Contemporary Romance

Witches Anonymous Step 1

Jingle Hells, WA Step 2

Wicked Souls, WA Step 3

Dark Moon Lilith, Witches Anonymous Step 4

Dancing With the Devil, Witches Anonymous Step 5

Devil's Due, Witches Anonymous Step 6

Dirty Deeds, Witches Anonymous Step 7

Wicked Wedding, Witches Anonymous Step 8

Urban Fantasy

Revenge Is Sweet, Kali Sweet Urban Fantasy Series, Book 1

Sweet Chaos, Kali Sweet Urban Fantasy Series, Book 2

Sweet Soldier, Kali Sweet Urban Fantasy Series, Book 3

Sweet Curse, Kali Sweet Urban Fantasy Series, Book 4

Paranormal Romantic Suspense

Soul Survivor, Moon Water Series, Book 1

Soul Protector, Moon Water Series, Book 2

Cozy Mysteries (writing as Nyx Halliwell)

Sister Witches Of Raven Falls Mystery Series

Of Potions and Portents

Of Curses and Charms

Of Stars and Spells

Of Spirits and Superstition

Confessions of a Closet Medium Cozy Mystery Series

Pumpkins & Poltergeists

Magic & Mistletoe

Hearts & Haunts

Vows & Vengeance

Once Upon a Witch Cozy Mystery Series

If the Cursed Shoe Fits (Cinder)

Beastly Book of Spells (Belle)

Poisoned Apple Potion (Snow) - only available in the Black Cat Crossing box set which is FREE when you sign up for the Whiskered Mysteries newsletter!

Red Hot Wolfie (Ruby)

Hexed Hair Day (Rapunzel)

MEET MISTY

USA TODAY Bestselling Author Misty Evans has published over seventy novels and writes romantic suspense, urban fantasy, and paranormal romance. Under her pen name, Nyx Halliwell, she also writes cozy mysteries.

When not reading or writing, she embraces her inner gypsy and loves music, movies, and hanging out with her husband, twin sons, and three spoiled puppies. She's a crafter at heart and has far too many projects to finish.

Don't want to miss a single adventure? Visit www.mistyevansbooks.com to find out ALL the news!

Check out her humorous pen name Nyx Halliwell for magical mysteries https://www.nyxhalliwell.com .

LETTER FROM MISTY

Hello Beautiful Reader!

Thank you for reading this story! It is an honor and a privilege to write stories for you.

I hope you enjoyed this book, and I'd like to ask a favor – would you mind leaving a review at your favorite retailer? I'd really appreciate it, and reviews help other readers find books they will love too.

If you'd like to learn about my other books, sales, and special promotions, please sign up for my newsletter at www.readmistyevans.com.

Grab special edition box sets and get new releases before they come out at retailers by visiting my direct buy website www.mistyevansbooks.com. I have sales and offer NEW RELEASES early and at a discount!! Check it out.

I also have a holistic business, Soul Healing With Misty, and invite you to check out my website www.crystalswithmisty.com for information on my services.

Last but not least, if you enjoy clean, cozy mysteries, visit my pen name www.nyxhalliwell.com to see those books!

Thank you and happy reading!

Misty